"Not that the story need be long, but it
will take a long while to make it short."
— Henry David Thoreau

Double/Double

Michael Richardson is the editor of *Mad-
dened by Mystery*, the first anthology of
Canadian detective fiction and with the poet
John Robert Colombo, the co-editor of an
anthology of Canadian tales of horror, *Not
To Be Taken At Night*, and *We Stand On
Guard: Poems & Songs of Canadians in Battle*. He lives in Toronto with his wife, an
identical twin, and his daughter, a palindrome.

Double/Double

Edited by

Michael Richardson

Penguin Books

Penguin Books Canada Ltd., 2801 John Street, Markham, Ontario, Canada L3R 1B4
Penguin Books Ltd., Harmondsworth, Middlesex, England
Penguin Books, 40 West 23rd Street, New York, New York 10010 U.S.A.
Penguin Books Australia Ltd., Ringwood, Victoria, Australia
Penguin Books (N.Z.) Ltd., Private Bag, 182-190 Wairau Road, Auckland 10,
New Zealand

First published by Penguin Books Canada Limited, 1987

Story credits on page vi constitute an extension of the copyright page.

Manufactured in Canada

Canadian Cataloguing in Publication Data

Main entry under title:

Double/double

(Penguin short fiction)
ISBN 0-14-010009-1

1. Doubles in literature. 2. Short stories.
I. Richardson, Michael, 1946-   . II. Series.

PN6120.95.D65D68 1987   808.83'872   C87-093155-5

Appropriately, for
Jeannie and Hannah

---

*For double the vision my eyes do see
And a double vision is always with me.*

William Blake

Double/Double

Contents

Acknowledgements   xi

Introduction   xiii

George D. Painter
  Meeting with a Double   xix

Hans Christian Andersen
  The Shadow   1

Ruth Rendell
  The Double   17

Tommaso Landolfi
  Gogol's Wife   35

Jorge Luis Borges
  August 25, 1983   51

John Barth
  Petition   59

Paul Bowles
  You Are Not I   77

Graham Greene
  The Case for the Defence   91

Susan Sontag
  The Dummy   99

Brian W. Aldiss
  The Expensive Delicate Ship   111

Alberto Moravia
  Doubles   121

Eric McCormack
  Twins   131

Julio Cortázar
  The Distances: The Diary of Alina Reyes   139

Algernon Blackwood
  Two in One   153

Adolfo Bioy Casares
  In Memory of Pauline   165

Acknowledgements

It is a pleasure to acknowledge the support of friends John and Ruth Colombo who as always gave freely of their time, suggestions, and hospitality. I am especially grateful to Catherine Lalande and Stuart Ross. Thanks also to friends Rob and Lise Van der Bleek, Jim and Nancy Arnot, Ernest Liptak, David Harlow, Billy Dreiger, Ross Snook, Joan and Jude Telford, and Philip Singer. I wish to thank Alberto Manguel for his suggestions, which led me to envision the imaginary double of this book; Cynthia Good of Penguin Books Canada Ltd., who first showed delight in the idea of this collection; and my editor Catherine Yolles, whose enthusiasm and contributions were inestimable. To my wife, Jeannie, who is an identical twin, and daughter Hannah, whose name is a palindrome, I dedicate this book for "other" reasons.

Over a period of time I consulted a large number of books and essays on the theme of the *doppelgänger*: Jorge Luis Borges's *Book of Imaginary Beings* (1969) and Robert Rogers's *A Psychoanalytic Study of the Double in Literature* (1970) did much to inspire this collection. Invaluable were Carl F. Keppler's *The Literature of the Second Self* (1972), Masao Miyoshi's *The Divided Self: A Perspective on the Literature of the Double* (1970), and James B. Twitchell's *Dreadful Pleasures: An Anatomy of Modern Horror* (1985), as were various writings on the theme by Robert Alter, Otto Rank, Claire Rosenfield, and Albert J. Guerard. For their writings on language and especially anagrams and palindromes I acknowledge Dmitri A. Borgmann and John Barth, and for their interviews and articles on various writers collected here I thank Diana Cooper-Clark, Evelyn Picon Garfield, Christopher Hitchens, and Jay McInerney. I drew especially on Eric Maple's essay on doubles in *Man, Myth and Magic*; A.E. Crawley's essay on same in *The Encyclopedia of Religion and Ethics* (1908–26); Colin Wilson's writings, especially his Village Press pamphlet on Borges; and Nandor Fodor's *Encyclopaedia of Psychic Science* (1966).

Introduction

There is a legend that somewhere in the world every person has a double. Stimulated by reflections in mirrors, surfaces of still lakes, twins, and the concept of the soul, the idea of the Double is universal. The ancient Egyptians believed that not just humans but all things—trees, boats, stones, and knives— had their precise duplicate, the *ka*. The North American Iroquois believe there is an ideal counterpart to each individual, a perfect model or type, the *oiaron*. The Dayaks of Sarawak, near Borneo, see their soul as a small figure resembling the person in every respect; they call it *bruwa*, meaning "two."

Sometimes the double has a sinister aspect. Throughout the world, superstitions surround the reflection and the shadow, linking them in uncanny ways to the soul: the Zulu fear looking into a pool of water, since their spirit may be captured; at a Chinese funeral, care is taken that no mourner's shadow be trapped inside the coffin; and in many Western countries it is still customary to cover mirrors during a funeral wake—lest the soul of the departed enter the living who are reflected therein. In England, folklore has it that on St. Mark's Eve one may see from the church porch all those who are to die during the course of the year. The idea of meeting oneself is then ominous, presaging death.

The names for the double are legion: in Scotland the apparition known as a *wraith* is the double of a person seen shortly before death; more telling is the Scottish *fetch*, who comes to fetch one to one's death. The *task* and *fye* of the British Isles are reflected in the *fylgja* or follower in Norse lore; its opposite is the *vardøger*, or forerunner, a phantasm who precedes the person. Catching another person's shadow is viewed as a talisman in some cultures. In *The Golden Bough* Sir James George Frazer cites many examples of shadows built into foundations to strengthen edifices. On the island of Lesbos a builder merely casts a stone at a passer-by's shadow in order to capture its good effects. If no man or beast should pass there was little problem, for as Frazer informs us, "Not long ago there were still shadow-traders whose business it was to provide architects with the shadows necessary for securing their walls."

It's in literature that the *doppelgänger*, or double-walker, is most often found. First introduced by the Romantic writer Jean Paul, nineteenth-century writing holds a profusion of *doppelgängers*, an expression perhaps of the heightened awareness of self among the increasingly urbanized middle class. James Hogg's *The Private Memoirs and Confessions of a Justified Sinner* appeared in 1824; E.T.A. Hoffman's melo-drama *Die Doppelgänger* appeared two years later. In Poe's "William Wilson" and Wilde's *The Picture of Dorian Gray*, the double serves as the protagonist's conscience. These and Stevenson's *Dr Jekyll and Mr Hyde*, Well's *The Island of Dr Moreau*, and Stoker's *Dracula* all explore the duality of hu-man nature, at once bestial and sublime. Perhaps Darwin's new theories of evolution served to fuel such speculation. In any case, it is worth noting that all these "monsters" were good Victorian gentlemen: even Count Dracula had, by day, a respectable London address (347, Piccadilly) and a taste for cricket!

If the *doppelgänger* fascinated nineteenth-century authors, as this anthology reflects, many writers of this century are haunted by the idea of the shadow. Leslie Fiedler's *The Second Stone*, Howard Nemerov's *Federigo* and Brian Moore's *The Mangan Inheritance* utilize the theme with virtuosity, and Nathalie Sarraute includes the motif as a dialogue between two selves in *Between Life and Death* and *Childhood*. A major theme of the contemporary novel is the search for identity, and not surprisingly, many writers have been drawn to reexamine the *doppelgänger* in this context. Preeminent among them is Vladimir Nabokov, despite his disclaimer that "the Doppelgänger subject is a frightful bore." In his novel *Despair*, a German chocolatier encounters a tramp he concludes to be his double and exchanges identities with him; in *The Eye*, the elusive protagonist Smurov assumes multiple identities that mirror the people around him; *Pale Fire* is likewise rife with shadows, mirrors, and *double-entendres*. Nabokov evidently agreed with the servant in Dostoevski's novel *The Double*: "Nice people don't live falsely and don't have doubles." But nice people are not especially interesting to write about. It is interesting to note that one of the finest literary explorations of the theme of the *doppelgänger*, Oscar Wilde's *The Picture of Dorian Gray* where Dorian stabs his portrait and meets his death, was inspired by a painting. In 1887, the Canadian artist Frances Richards painted Oscar Wilde's portrait (sadly, but perhaps not surprisingly, long since disappeared); the sitting over, Mr Wilde observed, "What a tragic thing it is, this portrait will never grow older, and I shall."

Freud explained the *doppelgänger* motif as the projection and diffusion of infantile desires that slip by the censoring superego, enabling the double to act independently of the central self. Thus, as Otto Rank suggests, the double links desire to fantasy. Ghosts, vampires, werewolves, dolls of necromancy and voodoo, the golem and its modern counterpart, the robot, are all examples of doubles; so too are such examples of fragmentation of the mind as Herman Hesse's *Steppenwolf* and the celebrated case study of multiple personality, *The Three Faces of Eve*. In *The Nazi Doctors: Medical Killing and the Psychology of Genocide*, Robert J. Lifton has recently theorized that it was the phenomenon of doubling which enabled Nazi doctors to perform the horrors at Auschwitz. The formation of a second, relatively autonomous self, the Auschwitz self, enabled the "ordinary" man to participate in evil.

If writers have given us many doppelgängers, perhaps this is because they seem disposed to meet them. Johann Wolfgang von Goethe wrote of the meeting with his double in *Aus Meinem Leben*:

> I rode now on the footpath toward Drusenheim, and there one of the strangest presentiments surprised me. I saw myself coming to meet myself, on the same way, on horseback, but in a garment such as I had never worn. It was of light grey mingled with gold. As soon as I had aroused myself from this dream, the vision entirely disappeared. Remarkable, nevertheless, it is that eight years afterward I found myself on the same road, intending to visit Frederika once more, and in the same garment which I had dreamed about and which I now wore, not out of choice but by accident. This wonderful hallucination had a quieting effect on me.

Shelley declared, a few days before his death by drowning, that he had met his double on the lake while boating. In 1889, Guy de Maupassant, nearing paralysis and death, was sitting at his desk when he thought he heard the door open. He turned and, to his surprise, saw his double enter, sit down, and, burying its head in its hands, begin to dictate what he himself was writing. Eerily, de Maupassant foreshadowed this experience in "The Horla," where the protagonist is gradually taken over by a vampiric other self.

If, as the Egyptians believed, all things have a double, we may not omit words: palindromes and anagrams both reflect the *doppelgänger* motif. There are palindrome sentences, which read the same backwards as forwards: "Able was I ere I saw Elba," and the palindromic verses:

> *Dog as a devil deified,*
> *Deified lived as a God.*

But it is to Vietnam that we must turn to find real palindromic poetry. Poet John Balaban tells of complex oral poems which, in strict metre, read forwards as a poem in Chinese and backwards as a poem in demotic Vietnamese, both perfectly coherent!

The character of an anthology is cast as much by excluding certain well-known stories as by embracing those less known. If the reader balks at not finding familiar stories of the *doppelgänger*, perhaps this disappointment can be offset by a brief description of the imagined *doppelgänger* of this volume. It is a battered old book, bound in red buckram, its stiff leather binding projecting considerably beyond the yellowing pages. The frontispiece reproduces Rossetti's painting "How They Met Themselves"; the text is prefaced by Alfred de Musset's poem, "La Nuit de Décembre." The contents read:

The Doubles .... E.T.A. Hoffman
The Horla .... Guy de Maupassant
William Wilson .... Edgar Allan Poe
Monsieur du Mirror .... Nathaniel Hawthorne
Those Extraordinary Twins .... Mark Twain
The Mirror and the Magistrate .... G.K. Chesterton
Bartleby the Scrivener .... Herman Melville
The Secret Sharer .... Joseph Conrad
The Foundling .... Heinrich von Kleist
The Jolly Corner .... Henry James

The forerunner or *vardóger* of the book you hold before you, it served as inspiration for the present selection.

Julio Cortázar has proposed that the experience of reading a short story should be similar to that of writing it. After immersion, the reader emerges from the tale, "as if from an act of love, exhausted and oblivious to the surrounding world, to which he returns little by little with a surprised look of slow recognition, many times of relief and other times of resignation." After immersion in the following stories, the reader will return, haunted by a sense of the shadow which these stories will continue to cast. Beware, lest they take thy shadow. . . !

Michael Richardson
Port Rowan/Toronto, 1987

Meeting with a Double
George D. Painter

When George began to climb all unawares
He saw a horrible face at the top of the stairs.

The rats came tumbling down the planks,
Pushing past without a word of thanks.

The rats were thin, the stairs were tall,
But the face at the top was worst of all.

It wasn't the ghost of his father or mother.
When they are laid there's always another.

It wasn't the ghost of people he knew.
It was worse than this, shall I tell you who?

It was himself, oh, what a disgrace.
And soon they were standing face to face.

At first they pretended neither cared,
But when they met, they stood and stared.

One started to smile and the other to frown.
And one moved up and the other moved down.

But which emerged and which one stays,
Nobody will know till the end of his days.

The Shadow
Hans Christian Andersen

Hans Christian Andersen

(Denmark, 1805–1875)

My first encounter with Hans Christian Andersen was seeing and hearing Danny Kaye sing "The Ugly Duckling" and "Thumbelina" in the children's musical *Hans Christian Andersen* (1952). Frank Loesser's sugary score did little to suggest Andersen's darker vision, but then neither did the Victorian translators of his tales. As translator Eric Christian Haugaard noted of his Victorian predecessors, "a kiss on the mouth in translation lands on the cheek." The Victorians reduced Andersen's work to the level of the nursery, removing not only the eroticism but the rhythms of literary prose.

Andersen did not write "fairy tales," nor, unlike the Brothers Grimm, did he collect folk tales. Instead, his stories spring from personal suffering. Born in a slum, Andersen was raised by an aunt who ran a brothel and a grandmother who kept the gardens of an asylum. In spite of poor spelling, he became successful as a writer, winning acclaim in 1835 with *Eventyr, fortalte for børn*, a collection of fantastic tales for children. In these stories the villains are not ogres and witches, but human frailties, especially vanity and indifference.

Although he fell in love several times (notably with singer Jenny Lind), Andersen never married, and suffered agonies of self-reproach over the "sin" of masturbation. It is this mentality that haunts such bittersweet tales as "The Little Tin Soldier," "The Little Fir Tree," and "The Shadow," the only nineteenth-century work included in this otherwise contemporary anthology. A classic *doppelgänger* story, it is strangely modern, presaging the sinister vision of Franz Kafka.

The Shadow

On the shores of the Mediterranean the sun really knows how to shine. It is so powerful that it tans the people a mahogany brown; and the young scholar who came from the north, where all the people are as white as bakers' apprentices, soon learned to regard his old friend with suspicion. In the south one stays inside during most of the day with the doors and shutters closed. The houses look as if everyone was asleep or no one was at home. The young foreigner felt as if he were in prison, and his shadow rolled itself up until it was smaller than it had ever been before. But as soon as the sun set and a candle lighted the room, out came the shadow again. It was truly a pleasure to watch it grow; up the wall it would stretch itself until its head almost reached the ceiling.

"The stars seem so much brighter here," thought the scholar, and he walked out onto his balcony where he stretched himself just as his shadow had done. And on all the balconies throughout the city people came out to enjoy the cool evening. Had the town appeared dead and deserted at noon, certainly now it was alive! People were flocking into the streets. The tailors and the shoemakers moved their workbenches outside; the women came with their straight-backed chairs to sit and gossip. Donkeys heavily laden with wares tripped along like little maids. Children were everywhere. They laughed, played, and sometimes cried as children will do, for children can run so fast that they are not certain whether it is a tragedy or a comedy they are enacting. And the lights! Thousands of lamps burned like so many falling stars. A funeral procession, led by little choir boys in black and white, passed with mournful but not sad-looking people following the black-draped horse and wagon. The church bells were ringing. "This is life!" thought the young foreigner, and he tried to take it all in.

Only the house directly across from his own was as quiet now as it had been at midday. The street was very narrow and the opposite balcony was only a few yards away. Often he stood and stared at it, but no one ever came out. Yet there were flowers there and they seemed to be flourishing, which meant that they were cared for or else the sun would long since have withered them. "Yes," he concluded, "they must be watered by someone." Besides, the shutters were opened, and while he never saw any light, he sometimes heard music. The scholar thought this music "exquisite," but that may be only because all young northerners think everything "exquisite" the first time they are in the south.

He asked his landlord if he knew who lived across the street, but the old man replied that he did not and, in fact, had never seen anyone enter or leave. As for the music, he could hardly express how terrible he thought it. "It's as if someone were practicing," he said. "The same piece, over and over and over again! And it's never played all the way through! It's unbearable!"

One night the young foreigner, who slept with his balcony door open, awakened with a start. A breeze had lifted his drapes so that he caught a glimpse of the opposite balcony. The flowers were ablaze with the most beautiful colors and in their midst stood a lovely maiden. For an instant the scholar closed his eyes to make sure that he had had them open. In a single leap he was standing in front of the drapes. Cautiously, he parted them; but the girl had vanished, the light had disappeared, and the flowers looked as they always did. The door, however, had been left open, and from far inside he could hear music; its gentle strains seemed to cast a spell over him, for never before had he taken such delight in his own thoughts. How does one get into that apartment? he wondered; and he perused the street below. There was no private entrance whatever, only a group of small shops; surely one could not enter a home through a store.

The next evening the scholar was sitting as usual on his balcony. From his room the lamp burned brightly, and since his shadow was very shy of light, it had stretched itself until it reached the opposite balcony. When the young man moved, his shadow moved. "I believe my shadow is the only living thing over there," he muttered. "See how it has sat down among the flowers. The balcony door is ajar. Now if my shadow were clever, it would go inside and take a look around; then it would come back and tell me what it had seen. Yes, you ought to earn your keep," he said jokingly. "Now go inside. Did you hear me? Go!" And he nodded to his shadow and his shadow nodded back at him. "Yes, go! But remember to come back again." There the scholar's conversation with his shadow ended. The young man rose, and the shadow on the opposite balcony rose; the young man turned around and the shadow also turned around; but then there happened something that no one saw. The shadow went through the half-open door of the other balcony, while the scholar went into his own room and closed the drapes behind him.

The next morning on his way to the café where he had his

breakfast and read the newspapers, the scholar discovered that he had no shadow. "So it really went away last night!" he marveled. More than anything else, the young man was embarrassed; people were certain to notice, and might demand that he explain or, worse than that, might make up explanations of their own. He returned at once to his room and there he remained for the rest of the day. That evening he walked out onto his balcony for a bit of fresh air. The light streamed from behind him as it had on the evening before. He sat down, stood up, stretched himself; still there was no shadow, and though it was doubtful that anyone could see him, he hurried inside again almost immediately.

But in the warm countries everything grows much faster than it does in the north, and less than a week had passed before a shadow began to sprout from the scholar's feet. "The old one must have left its roots behind, what a pleasant surprise!" he thought happily. Within a month he walked the streets unconcerned; his shadow, though a little small, was quite respectable. During the long trip, for the scholar was going home, it continued to grow until even a very big man, which the scholar was not, would not have complained about its size.

Settled once more in his own country, the scholar wrote books about all that is true and beautiful and good. The days became years. The scholar was now a philosopher; and the years became many. One evening when he was sitting alone in his room there was a very gentle knock at the door.

"Come in," he called. But no one came, so the philosopher opened the door himself. Before him stood the thinnest man that he had ever seen but, judging from his clothes, a person of some importance. "Whom do I have the honor of addressing?" the philosopher asked.

"I thought as much," replied the stranger. "You don't recognize me, now that I have a body of my own and clothes to boot. You never would have believed that you would meet your old shadow again. Things have gone well for me since we parted. If need be, I can buy my freedom!" The shadow jiggled its purse, which was filled with gold pieces, and touched the heavy gold chain that it wore around its neck. On all of its fingers were diamond rings, and every one was genuine.

"I must be dreaming!" exclaimed the philosopher. "What is happening?"

"Well, it isn't something that happens every day," said the shadow, "but then, you're not an ordinary person. Nobody knows that better than I do, didn't I walk in your first footsteps? . . . As soon as you found that I could stand alone in the world, you let me go. The results are obvious. Without bragging, I can say few could have done better. . . . Of late, a longing has come over me to talk with you before you die— you must die, you know. Besides, I wanted to see this country again, only a rogue does not love his native land. . . . I know that you have a new shadow. If I owe you or it anything, you will be so kind as to tell me."

"Is it really you?" cried the philosopher. "It's so incredible! I wouldn't have believed that one's shadow could come back to one as a human being!"

"Tell me how much I owe you," insisted the shadow. "I hate to be in debt."

"How can you talk like that?" replied the philosopher. "What debt could there be to pay? Be as free as you wish! I am only happy to see you again. And I rejoice in your good luck. Sit down, old friend," he invited most cordially. "Tell me how all this came about, and what you saw that night in the house across the street."

"Yes, I will tell you about it," agreed the shadow, and sat down. "But first you must promise me that you will never tell anyone that I once was your shadow. I've been thinking of becoming engaged; after all, I am quite rich enough to support a large family."

"Don't give it another moment's thought," the philosopher said. "I will never tell anyone who you really are. Here is my hand on it. A man is no better than his word."

"And a word is a shadow," remarked the shadow, because it could not speak otherwise.

It was really amazing, how human the shadow appeared. It was dressed completely in black, but everything was of the finest quality from its patent leather boots to its hat of the softest felt. The gold chain and the rings have already been described, but one's eye fell upon them so often that one cannot help mentioning them again. Yes, the shadow was well dressed, and clothes make the man.

"Now I shall begin," announced the shadow, and it stamped its boots as hard as it could on the philosopher's new shadow, which was curled up like a poodle at the feet of the man. Perhaps it did this because it hoped to attach the philosopher's shadow to itself, or maybe just because it was arrogant; but the new shadow did not appear ruffled. It lay perfectly still and listened, for it too wanted to know how one could be free and become one's own master.

"Do you know who lived in the house across the street?" asked the shadow. "That's the best of all, it was Poetry! I was there for three weeks, and that is just as edifying as having lived three thousand years and read everything that's ever been composed or written. This I say, and what I say is true! I have seen all and I know all!"

"Poetry!" cried the philosopher. "Yes . . . yes. She is often a hermit in the big cities. I saw her myself once, but only for a short moment and my eyes were drowsy from sleep. She was standing on the balcony and it was as if the northern lights were shining around her. . . . Go on, go on! There you were on the balcony; then you walked through the doorway and . . . and . . ."

"I was in the entrance hall. That's what you sat looking at all the time, the vestibule. There was no lamp in there, and that's why from the outside the apartment appeared dark. But there was a door. It opened onto another room, which opened onto another, which opened onto another. There was a long row of rooms and anterooms before one reached the innermost where Poetry lived. And these were ablaze with more than enough light to kill a shadow, so I never saw the maiden up close. I was cautious and patient, and that is the same as being virtuous."

"Come, come," commanded the philosopher curtly. "Tell me what you saw."

"Everything! And I'll tell you about it, but first ... It has nothing whatever to do with pride, but out of respect to my accomplishments, not to speak of my social position, I wish you wouldn't address me so familiarly."

"Forgive me!" exclaimed the philosopher. "It is an old habit, and they are the hardest to get rid of. But you are quite right, and I'll try to remember. . . . Please do continue, for I am immensely interested."

"Everything! I have seen all, and I know all!"

"I beg you to tell me about the innermost room where Poetry dwelled. Was it like the beech forest in spring? Was it like the interior of a great cathedral? Or was it like the heavens when one stands on a mountaintop?"

"Everything was there!" replied the shadow. "Of course, I never went all the way in. The twilight of the vestibule suited me better, and from there I had an excellent view. I saw everything and I know all. I was at the court of Poetry, in the entrance hall."

"But what did you see?" urged the philosopher. "Did Thor and Odin walk those halls? Did Achilles and Hector fight their battles again? Or did innocent children play there and tell of their dreams?"

"I am telling you that I was there. And you understand, I saw everything that there was to see. You could not have stayed there and remained a human being, but it made a human being of me! I quickly came to understand my innermost nature, that part of me which from birth can claim kinship to Poetry. When I lived with you, I didn't even think about such things. You'll remember that I was always larger at sunrise and at sunset, and that I was more noticeable in the moonlight than you were. Still, I had no understanding of my nature; that did not come until I was in the vestibule, and then I became a human being.

"I was fully mature when I came out; by then you had already left the south. Being human made me ashamed to go around as I was; I needed boots, clothes, and all the other trimmings that make a man what he is. So there was nothing else for me to do but hide. . . . I wouldn't say this to anyone but you, and you mustn't mention it in any of your books. . . . I hid under the skirts of the woman who sold gingerbread men in the market. Luckily, she never found out how much her petticoats concealed. I came out only in the evening; then I would walk around in the moonlight, stretching myself up the walls to get the kinks out of my back. Up and down the streets I went, peeping through the windows of the attics as well as the drawing rooms. And I saw what no one ever sees, what no one ever should see! It's really a horrible world, and I wouldn't be human if it weren't so desirable. I saw things that ought to be unthinkable; and these were not only done by husbands and wives, but by parents and the sweet, innocent children! I saw," said the shadow, "I saw everything that man must not know, but what he most ardently wishes to know—his neighbor's evil! If I had written a newspaper, everyone would have read it; but instead I wrote directly to the persons themselves, and I wreaked havoc in every city that I came to. People feared me so much and were so fond of me! The universities gave me honorary degrees, the tailors gave me clothes, and the women said that I was handsome. In a word, each donated what he could, and so I became the man that I am. . . . But it is getting late, and I must say good-by.

Here is my card. I live on the sunnier side of the street and am always home when it rains."

"How strange!" remarked the philosopher after the shadow had left.

The years and the days passed, and the shadow came again. "How are things going?" it asked.

"Oh," replied the philosopher, "I have been writing about all that is true and beautiful and good, but no one cares to hear about anything like that, and I am terribly disappointed because those are the things that are dear to me."

"Well, they aren't to me," said the shadow. "I've been concentrating on gaining weight, and that there's some point in. You don't understand the world, that's what's the matter with you. You ought to travel. I am going on a trip this summer, would you like to join me? If you would like to travel as my shadow it would be a pleasure to have you along. I'll pay for your trip!"

"You go too far!" retorted the philosopher.

"It all depends how you look at it. The trip will do you good and, traveling as my shadow, you'll have all your expenses paid by me."

"Monstrous!" shouted the philosopher.

"But that's the way of the world, and it isn't going to change," said the shadow, and left.

Matters did not improve for the philosopher; on the contrary, sorrow and misery had attached themselves to his coattails. For the most part, whenever he spoke of the true and the beautiful and the good, it was like setting roses before a cow. Finally he became seriously ill. "You look like a shadow of your former self," people would say, and when he heard these words a shiver went down his spine.

"You ought to go to a health resort," suggested the shadow when it came to visit him again. "There's no other alternative. I will take you along for old time's sake. I'll pay the expenses, and you'll talk and try to amuse me along the journey. I'm going to a spa, myself, because my beard won't grow. That's a disease too, you know, because beards are a necessity. If you're sensible, you'll accept. We'll travel as friends."

And so they traveled, the shadow as master and the master as shadow, for whether they were being driven in a coach, riding horseback, or simply walking, they were always side by side and the shadow kept itself a little in the fore or in the rear, according to the direction of the sun. It knew how to create the impression that it was the superior. The philosopher, however, was not aware of any of this. He had a kind heart, which did not even have a guest room reserved for envy. The journey was not yet over when the philosopher suggested to the shadow, "Now that we're traveling companions—and when you consider the fact that we've grown up together, shouldn't we call each other by first names? It makes for a much pleasanter atmosphere."

"There's something in what you say," began the shadow, who now was the real master. "You have spoken frankly, and what you have said was well meant; therefore, I ought to be honest with you. As a philosopher, you know how strange nature can be. Some people cannot bear to have a rough piece of material next to their bodies, and others can't hear a nail scratching on glass without it upsetting their nervous systems. Well, I would have the same feeling if you were to call me by my first name. I would have the feeling that I was being pressed to the ground, as if my relationship to you had never changed. You understand it's merely a feeling, it has nothing whatever to do with pride. But I could call you by your first name and satisfy half of your request."

From then on, the shadow always spoke and referred to the philosopher by his first name. "He goes too far," thought the man. "He's hardly civil to me." But when one is poor, one does more thinking than speaking.

At last they arrived at the famous resort where people came from all over the world to be cured. Among the guests was a beautiful princess who suffered from seeing too clearly, which is a very painful disease. She noticed at once that one of the new arrivals was very different from everyone else. He had come to make his beard grow, she was told. "But that's not the real reason," she muttered to herself. And to satisfy her curiosity, she went right up and spoke to the stranger, for the daughter of a king need not stand on ceremony with anyone.

"Your trouble is that you cannot cast a shadow," the princess announced.

"Your Royal Highness is getting well!" exclaimed the shadow. "I know that you suffered from seeing too clearly, but you must be getting over it. You show signs of perfect health. . . . I grant you that it is a very unusual one, but I do have a shadow. Other people have just ordinary shadows, but I despise the ordinary. You know how one dresses one's servants so that their livery is finer than one's own clothes; well, I let my shadow pretend that he is human. As you can see, I have even bought him a shadow. It was very expensive, but I am fond of doing the original."

"What!" thought the princess. "Have I really been cured? This is the finest spa there is. How fortunate I am to be born in the time when these marvelous waters were discovered. . . . But just because I am well is no reason to leave. I'm enjoying myself here. That stranger interests me, I hope his beard won't grow too quickly."

That night there was a grand ball that everyone attended, and the shadow danced with the princess. The princess was light on her toes, but the shadow was even lighter; such a graceful partner she had never had before. They discovered that he had once visited her country while she was abroad. There, too, the shadow had peeped through all of the windows, those that faced the street and those that did not. He had seen both this and that; and he knew how to tell about some of what he had seen and how to hint at the rest, which was even more impressive. The princess was astounded. She had never spoken to anyone who was so worldly wise, and out of respect for what he knew, she danced with him again.

The next time they danced together the princess fell in love. The shadow noticed the sudden change with relief. "She's finally been cured of seeing too clearly," he thought.

The princess would have confessed her feelings immediately if she hadn't been so prudent. She thought of her realm and of the people she ruled. "He knows well the ways of the world, that's a good sign," she commented silently. "He dances well, that is also a virtue. But is he really educated, for that is very important? I'd better test him." Then she began to ask the shadow questions so difficult that she herself did not know the answers.

An expression of confusion came over the shadow's face. "You cannot answer!" exclaimed the princess.

"I learned the answers to questions like that in childhood," said the shadow. "I believe that even my shadow, who is sitting over there by the door, could respond correctly."

"Your shadow! That really would be remarkable!"

"I can't say for certain," continued the shadow. "I just wouldn't be surprised if he could. After all, he's never done anything but follow me around and listen to what I say. Yes," he cried in a sudden burst of enthusiasm, "I believe he will be able to answer you! . . . But, Your Royal Highness, if you will allow me to make a suggestion. My shadow is so proud of being thought to be human, if Your Royal Highness wishes to create the right atmosphere, so that the shadow will be able to do his best, please treat him as if he were a man."

"I'd prefer it that way," said the king's daughter, and she joined the philosopher, who was alongside the door. She questioned him about the sun and the moon, and about the human race, both inside and out; and he answered every query both cleverly and politely.

"What must the man be worth, if his shadow is so wise!" thought the princess. "It would be a blessing for my people if I chose him for my husband. I shall do it!"

The shadow was very amenable. It agreed without hesitation that their plans must not be revealed until the princess had returned home. "I will not even tell my shadow," he said, while he thought how admirably the world had been created.

Not long after they came to the land which the princess ruled whenever she was there.

"My good friend," the shadow began to the philosopher. "Now that I am as happy and as powerful as anyone can hope to be, I'd like to share my good fortune with you. You may live with me always, here in the castle; you may drive with me in the royal coach; and you will be paid one hundred thousand gold pieces a year. In return, all I ask is that you let everyone call you a shadow; that you never admit to anyone that you have ever been a human being; and that once a year, when I sit on the balcony so that the people can pay me homage, you lie at my feet as a shadow should. . . . I might as well tell you that I am marrying the princess, and the wedding is tonight."

"No, this cannot happen!" cried the philosopher. "I don't want to do it, and I won't! You are a fraud! I will tell everything! You've fooled both the people and the princess; but now I will tell them that I am a human being and that you are only my shadow, who's been masquerading as a man!"

"No one will believe you," warned the shadow. "Now be reasonable or I'll call the guard."

"I intend to ask for an audience with the princess," replied the philosopher.

"But I will speak with her first," said the shadow, "and you will be imprisoned."

The shadow's threat very quickly became a reality, for the royal sentry knew whom the princess had chosen to be her husband.

"You are shivering," remarked the princess as soon as he entered her chambers. "You must not get sick this evening, not for the wedding!"

"I've just had the most horrible experience that one can have," replied the shadow. "Imagine! . . . Oh, how fragile a shadow's brain must be! . . . Imagine, my shadow has gone mad. He believes he is a man. And that I . . . that I am his shadow!"

"How dreadful!" she exclaimed. "He isn't running around loose, I hope."

"No, no, he's not," he said softly. "I am so afraid he will never get well."

"Poor shadow," continued the princess. "He must be suffering terribly. It would really be kinder to free him from that particle of life he has. Yes, the more I think about it, the more convinced I am that it's necessary for him to be done away with. . . . Quietly, of course."

"It seems so cruel," said the shadow, "when I think of how loyal a servant it was," and a sound resembling a sigh escaped from the shadow's lips.

"How noble you are!" exclaimed the princess.

That night the whole city was brilliantly lighted. The cannons were shot off. Bum! Bum! Bum! The soldiers presented arms. Oh, what a wedding it was! The shadow and the princess came out onto the balcony, and the people screamed, "Hurrah!"

The philosopher heard nothing of all of this, for they had already taken his life.

Translated from the Danish by Erik Christian Hangaard

Do you know where your
shadow is tonight?

The Double
Ruth Rendell

Ruth Rendell
(England, b. 1930)

Ruth Rendell is eminent in two categories of mystery writing. Francis Wyndham of the *Times Literary Supplement* observed, "Ruth Rendell's remarkable talent has been able to accommodate the rigid rules of the reassuring mystery story (where a superficial logic conceals a basic fantasy) as well as the wider range of the disturbing psychological thriller (where an appearance of nightmare overlays a scrupulous realism)." Her novels featuring sly, eccentric Inspector Reg Wexford are classic puzzlers, while her psychological thrillers (*The Face of Trespass, Demon in My View, A Judgement in Stone, The Lake of Darkness*) present a less ordered society. In 1986 she assumed the pseudonym Barbara Vine to display further versatility in *A Dark-Adapted Eye*.

It is only, in John Mortimer's view, the "ridiculous snobbery" of those critics who dismiss crime writing that has kept Rendell from acclaim as an important novelist. Few writers have treated rapists, mutilators, and child murderers with such humanity; her "monsters" are ordinary human beings, and in their very ordinariness lies the horror. Asked why she writes of such things, Rendell has said, "Not because I am working out any impulses. My work and daily life are two separate compartments of my mind."

Before the days of nice distinctions between genres and subgenres, horror and occult tales were considered mystery writing. The occult flavour of "The Double" (first published in *Ellery Queen's Mystery Magazine* as "A Meeting in the Park") is therefore not surprising. As in Rendell's psychological thrillers, the nightmare is grounded in a realistic moral—if living a double life is dangerous, then two-timing one's lover can be fatal.

The Double

Strange dishevelled women who had the air of witches sat round the table in Mrs Cleasant's drawing room. One of them, a notable medium, seemed to be making some sort of divination with a pack of Tarot cards. Later on, when it got dark, they would go on to table-turning. The aim was to raise up the spirit of Mr Cleasant, one year dead, and also perhaps, Peter thought with anger and disgust, to frighten Lisa out of her wits.

"Where are you going?" said Mrs Cleasant when Lisa came back with her coat on.

Peter answered for her. "I'm taking her for a walk in Holland Park, and then we'll have a meal somewhere."

"Holland Park?" said the medium. If a corpse could have spoken it would have had a voice like hers. "Take care, be watchful. That place has a reputation."

The witch women looked at her expectantly, but the medium had returned to her Tarot and was eyeing the Empress which she had brought within an inch or two of her long nose. Peter was sickened by the lot of them. Six months to go, he thought, and he'd take her out of this—this coven.

It was a Sunday afternoon in spring, and the air in the park was fresh and clean, almost like country air. Peter drew in great gulps of it, cleansing himself of the atmosphere of that drawing room. He wished Lisa would unwind, be less nervous and strung-up. The hand he wasn't holding kept going up to the charm she wore on a chain round her neck or straying out to knock on wood as they passed a fence.

Suddenly she said, "What did that woman mean about the park's reputation?"

"Some occult rubbish. How should I know? I hate that sort of thing."

"So do I," she said, "but I'm afraid of it."

"When we're married you'll never have to have any more to do with it. I'll see to that. God, I wish we could get married now or you'd come and live with me till we can."

"I can't marry you till I'm eighteen without Mummy's permission, and if I go and live with you they'll make me a ward of court."

"Surely not, Lisa."

"Anyway, there's only six months to wait. It's hard for me too. Don't you think I'd rather live with you than with Mummy?"

The childish rejoinder made him smile. "Come on, try and look a bit more cheerful. I want to take your photograph. If I can't have you, I'll have your picture." They had reached a sunny open space where he sat her on a log and told her to smile. He got the camera out of its case. "Don't look at those people, darling. Look at me."

It was a pity the man and the girl had chosen that moment to sit down on the wooden seat.

"Lisa!" he said sharply, and then he wished he hadn't, for her face crumpled with distress. He went up to her. "What's the matter now, Lisa?"

"Look at that girl," she said.

"All right. What about her?"

"She's exactly like me. She's my double."

"Nonsense. What makes you say that? Her hair's the same colour and you're about the same build, but apart from that, there's no resemblance. She's years older than you and she's . . ."

"Peter, you must see it! She might be my twin. Look, the man with her has noticed. He looked at me and said something to her and then they both looked."

He couldn't see more than a superficial similarity. "Well, supposing she were your double, which I don't for a moment admit, so what? Why get in such a state about it?"

"Don't you know about doubles? Don't you know that if you see your double, you're seeing your own death, you die within the year?"

"Oh, Lisa, come *on*. I never heard anything so stupid. This is more rubbish you've picked up from those crazy old witches. It's just sick superstition." But nothing he could say calmed her. Her face had grown white and her eyes troubled. Worried for her rather than angry, he put out his hand and helped her to her feet. She leant against him, trembling, and he saw she was clutching her amulet. "Let's go," he said. "We'll find another place to take your picture. Don't look at her if it upsets you. Forget her."

When they had gone off along the path, the man on the seat said to his companion, "Couldn't you really see that girl was the image of you?"

"I've already told you, no."

"Of course you look a good deal older and harder, I'll give you that."

"Thank you."

"But you're almost her double. Take away a dozen years and a dozen love affairs, and you'd *be* her double."

"Stephen, if you're trying to start another row, just say so and I'll go home."

"I'm not starting anything. I'm fascinated by an extraordinary phenomenon. Holland Park's known to be a strange place. There's a legend you can see your own double there."

"I never heard that."

"Nevertheless, my dear Zoe, it is so.

" 'The Magus, Zoroaster, my dead child,
Saw his own image walking in the garden.' "

"Who said that?"

"Shelley. Superstition has it that if you see your own image you die within the year."

She turned slowly to look at him. "Do you want me to die within the year, Stephen?"

He laughed. "Oh, you won't die. You didn't see her, she saw you. And it frightened her. He was taking her photograph, did you see? I wish I'd asked him to take one of you two together. Why don't we see if we can catch them up?"

"You know, you have a sick imagination."

"No, only a healthy curiosity. Come along now, if we walk fast we'll catch them up by the gate."

"If it amuses you," said Zoe.

Peter and Lisa didn't see the other couple approaching. They were walking with their arms round each other, and Peter had managed to distract her from the subject of her double by talking of their wedding plans. At the northern gate someone behind him called out, "Excuse me!" and he turned to see the man who had been sitting on the seat.

"Yes?" he said rather stiffly.

"I expect you'll think this is frightful cheek, but I saw you back there and I was absolutely—well, struck by the likeness between my girl friend and the young lady with you. There is a terrific likeness, isn't there?"

"I don't see it," said Peter, not daring to look at Lisa. What a beastly thing to happen! He felt dismay. "Frankly, I don't see any resemblance at all."

"Oh, but you must. Look, what I want is for you to do me

an enormous favour and take a picture of them together. Will you? Do say you will."

Peter was about to refuse, and not politely, when Lisa said, "Why not? Of course he will. It's such a funny coincidence, we ought to have a record of it."

"Good girl! We'd better introduce ourselves then, hadn't we? I'm Stephen Davidson and this is Zoe Conti."

"Lisa Cleasant and Peter Milton," said Peter, still half-stunned by Lisa's warm response.

"Hallo, Lisa and Peter. Lovely to know you. Now you two girls go and stand over there in that spot of sunshine . . ."

So Peter took the photograph and said he'd send Stephen and Zoe a copy when the film was developed. She gave him the address of the flat she and Stephen shared and he noted it was in the next street but one to his. They might have walked there together, which was what Stephen, remarking on this second coincidence, seemed to want. But seeing the tense, strained look in Lisa's eyes, Peter refused, and they separated in Holland Park Avenue.

"You didn't mind about not going with them, did you?" said Lisa.

"Of course not. I'd rather be alone with you."

"I'm glad," she said, and then, "I did it for you."

He understood. She had done it for him, to prove to him she could conquer those superstitious terrors. For his sake, because he wanted it, she would try. He took her in his arms and kissed her.

She leant against him. He could feel her heart beating. "I shan't tell anyone else about it," she said, and he knew she meant her mother and the witch women.

When the film was developed he didn't show it to her. Zoe and Stephen should have their copy and that would be an end of the whole incident. But when he was putting it into an envelope, he realized he would have to write a covering note, which was a bore as he didn't like writing letters. Besides, if

he was going to take it to the post, he might as well take it to
their home. This, one evening, he did.

He had no intention of going in. But as he was slipping the
envelope into the letter box, Zoe appeared behind him on the
steps.

"Come in and have a drink."

He couldn't think of an excuse, so he accepted. She led him
up two flights of stairs, looking at the photograph as she
went.

"So much for this fantastic likeness," she said. "Could you
ever see it?"

Peter said he couldn't, wondering how Lisa could have
been so silly as to fancy she had seen her double in this
woman of thirty, who tonight had a drawn and haggard look.
"It was mostly in your friend's imagination," he said as they
entered the flat. "We'll see what he says about it now."

For a moment she didn't answer. When her reply came it
was brusque. "He's left me."

Peter was embarrassed. "I'm sorry." He looked into her
face, at the eyes whose dark sockets were like bruises. "Are
you very unhappy?"

"I shan't take an overdose, if that's what you mean. We'd
been together for four years. It's hard to take. But I won't bore
you with it. Let's talk about something else."

Peter had only meant to stay half an hour, but the half-
hour grew into an hour, and when Zoe said she was going to
cook her dinner and would he stay and have it with her, he
agreed. She was interesting to talk to. She was a music thera-
pist, and she talked about her work and played records. When
they had finished their meal, a simple but excellent one, she
reverted to her own private life and told him something of her
long and fraught relationship with Stephen. But she spoke
without self-pity. And she could listen as well as talk. It
meant something to him to be able to confide in a mature
well-balanced woman who heard him out without interrup-

tion while he spoke of himself and Lisa, how they were going to be married when she was eighteen and when she would inherit half her dead father's fortune. Not, he said, that the money had anything to do with it. He'd have preferred her to be penniless. All he wanted was to get her away from that unhealthy atmosphere of dabbling with the occult, from that cloistral home where she was sheltered yet corrupted.

"What is she afraid of?" asked Zoe when he told her about the wood-touching and the indispensable amulet.

He shrugged. "Of fate? Of some avenging fury that resents her happiness?"

"Or of loss," said Zoe. "She lost her father. Perhaps she's afraid of losing you."

"That's the last thing she need be afraid of," he said.

It was midnight before he left. The next day he meant to tell Lisa where he had been. There were no secrets between them. But Lisa was nervous and uneasy—she and Mrs Cleasant had been to a spiritualist meeting—and he thought it unwise to raise once more a subject that was better forgotten. So he said nothing. After all, he would never see Zoe again.

But a month or so later, a month in which he and Lisa had been happy and tranquil together, he met the older girl by chance in the Portobello Road. While they talked, it occurred to him that he had eaten a meal in her flat and that he owed her dinner. He and Lisa would take her out to dinner. In her present mood, Lisa would like that, and it would be good for her to see, after the lapse of time, how her superstitiousness had led her into error. He put the invitation to Zoe who hesitated, then accepted when he explained it would be a threesome. Dinner, then, in a fortnight's time, and he and Lisa would call for her.

"I met that girl Zoe and asked her to have dinner with us. All right with you?"

The frightened child look came back into Lisa's face.

"Oh, no, Peter! I thought you understood, I don't ever want to see her again."

"But why not? You've seen the photograph, you've seen how silly those ideas of yours were. And Stephen won't be there. I know you didn't like him and neither did I. But they're not together any more. He's left her."

She shivered. "Let's not get to know her, Peter."

"I've invited her," he said. "I can't go back on that now."

When the evening came, Zoe appeared at her door in a long gown, her hair dressed on top of her head. She looked majestic, mysteriously changed.

"Where's Lisa?" she asked.

"She couldn't come. She and her mother are going on holiday to Greece at the end of the week and she's busy packing." Part of this was true. He said it confidently, as if it were wholly true. He couldn't take his eyes off the new transformed Zoe, and he was glad he had booked a table in an exclusive restaurant.

In the soft lamplight her youth had come back to her. And for the first time he was aware of the likeness between her and Lisa. The older and the younger sister, by a trickery of light and cosmetics and maybe of his own wistful imagination, had met in years and become twins. It might have been his Lisa who spoke to him across the table, across the silver and glass and the single rose in a vase, but a Lisa whom life and experience had matured. Never could Lisa have talked like this of books and music and travel, or listened to him so responsively or advised with such wisdom. He was sorry when the evening came to an end and he left her at her door.

Lisa seemed to have forgotten his engagement to dine with Zoe. She didn't mention it, so he didn't either. On the following morning she was to leave with her mother for the month's holiday the doctor had recommended for Mrs Cleasant's health.

"I wish I wasn't going," she said to Peter. "You don't know how I'll miss you."

"Shan't I miss you?"

"Take care of yourself. I'll worry in case anything happens to you. You mustn't laugh, but when my father was alive and went away from us, I used to listen to the news four or five times a day in case there was a plane crash or a disaster."

"You're the one that's going away, Lisa."

"It comes to the same thing." She put up her hand to the charm she wore. "I've got this, but you ... Would you take my four-leaved clover if I gave it to you?"

"I thought you'd given up all that nonsense," he said, and his disappointment in her soured their farewells. She kissed him good-bye with a kind of passionate sadness.

"Write to me," she said. "I'll write every day."

Her letters started coming at the end of the first week. They were the first he had ever had from her and they were like school essays written by a geography student, with love messages for the class teacher inserted here and there. They left him unsatisfied, a little peevish. He was lonely without her, but frightened of the image of her he carried with him. He needed someone with whom to talk it over and, after a few days of indecision, he telephoned Zoe. Ten minutes later he was in her flat, drinking her coffee and listening to her music. To be with her was a greater comfort than he had thought possible, for in the turn of her head, a certain way of hers of smiling, the way her hair grew from a widow's peak on her forehead, he caught glimpses of Lisa.

And yet on that occasion he said nothing of his fears but "I can't understand why I thought you and Lisa weren't alike."

"I didn't see it."

"It's almost overpowering, it's uncanny."

She smiled. "If it helps you to come and see me to get through the time while she's away, that's all right with me, Peter. I can understand that I remind you of her and that makes things easier for you."

"It isn't only that," he said. "You mustn't think it's only that."

She said no more. It wasn't her way to probe, to hold inquisitions, or to set an egotistical value on herself. But the next time they were together, he explained without being asked, and his explanation was appalling to him, the words more powerful and revealing than the thoughts from which they had sprung.

"It isn't true you remind me of Lisa. That's not it. It's that I see in you what she might become, only she never will."

"Who would want to be like me?"

"Everyone. Every young girl. Because you're what a woman should be, Zoe, clever and sane and kind and self-reliant and—beautiful."

"And if that's true," she said lightly, "though I disagree, why shouldn't Lisa become like that?"

"Because when she's eighteen she'll be rich, an heiress. She'll never have to work for her living or struggle or learn. We'll live in a house near her mother and she'll get like her mother, vain and neurotic, living on sleeping pills, spending all her time with spiritualists and getting involved in sick cults. When I look at you I don't see Lisa's double. I see her, an alternative she, if you like, thirteen years ahead in time if another path had been marked out for her in life. And at the same time I see you as you'd be if you'd led the sort of life she must and will lead."

"You can help her not to lead that life if you love her," said Zoe.

And then Lisa's letters stopped coming. A week went by without a letter. He had resolved, because of what was happening to him, not to see Zoe again. But she lived so near and he thought of her so often that he was unable to resist. He went to her and told a lie that he convinced himself might be the truth. Lisa was too young to have a firm and faithful love for anyone. Her letters had grown cold and had finally ceased to come. Zoe listened to him, to his urgent pursuasions, his comparison of his forsaken state with her own, and when he kissed her, she responded at first with doubts, then with an ardour born of her own loneliness. They made love. When, later, he asked her if he might stay the night, she said he could and he did.

After that, he spent every night with her. He hardly went home. When he did he found ten letters waiting for him on the doormat. Lisa and her mother had gone on to some Aegean island—the home of a mystic Mrs Cleasant longed to meet—where the posts were hazardous. He read the childish letters, the "darling Peter, I miss you, I'll never go away again" with impatience and with guilt, and then he went back to Zoe.

Why did he have to mention those letters to her? He wished he hadn't. It was for her wisdom and her honesty that he had wanted her, and now those very qualities were striking back at him.

"When is she coming home?"

"Next Saturday," he said.

"Peter, I don't know what you mean to do, leave me and marry her, or leave her and stay with me. But you must tell her about us, whatever you decide."

"I can't do that!"

"You must. Either way, you must. And if you mean to stay with me, what alternative have you?"

Stay with them both until he was sure, until he knew for certain. "You know I can't be without you, Zoe. But I can't tell her, not yet. She's such a child."

"You're going to marry that child. You love her."

"Do I?" he said. "I thought I did."

"I won't be a party to deceiving her, Peter. You must understand that. If you won't promise to tell her, I can't see you again."

Perhaps when he saw Lisa . . . He went across the park to her mother's house on the Sunday evening. The medium was there and another woman who looked like a participant in a

Black Mass, earnestly listening to Mrs Cleasant's account of the mystic and his investigations into the mysteries of the Great Pyramid. Lisa rushed into his arms, actually crying with happiness.

"This child has dreamed about you every night, Peter," said Mrs Cleasant with one of her weird faraway looks. "Such dreams she has had! Of course she's psychic like me. When we knew the posts were delayed I wanted her to get a message through to you by the Power of Thought, but she was unwilling."

"I knew you wouldn't like it," said Lisa. She sat on his knee, in his arms. Of course he couldn't tell her. In time, maybe, if he got their wedding postponed and cooled things and . . . But it was out of the question to tell her now.

He told Zoe he had. In order to see her again, he had to do that.

"How did she take it?"

"Oh, quite well," he lied. "A lot of men have been paying her attention on holiday. I think she's just beginning to realize I'm not the only man in the world."

"And she accepts—us?"

Why did she have to persist, why make it so painful for him? He spoke boldly but with an inner self-disgust.

"I daresay she sees it as a let-out for her own freedom."

She was convinced. The habitual truth-teller is reluctant to detect falsehood in others. "Of course I've only met her once, and then only for a few minutes. But I wonder if you weren't deceiving yourself, Peter, when you said she loved you so much. You aren't going to see her again?"

He said he wasn't. He said it was all over, they had parted. But the enormity of what he had done appalled him. And when next he was with Lisa he found himself telling her all over again, and meaning it, how much he loved her and longed to take her away. Was he going to sacrifice that childish passionate love for a woman five years older than himself? They were, in many ways, so alike. Suppose, in time to come, he grew tired of the one and regretted the other? Yet, that night, he went back to Zoe.

With a skilful but frightening intrigue, he divided his time between the one and the other. It wasn't too difficult. Social— and occult—demands were always being made on Lisa. Zoe believed him when he said he had been kept late at work. Autumn came, and it was still going on, this double life. His need for, his dependence on, Zoe intensified and he had begun to resent every moment he spent away from her. But Lisa and her mother had fixed his wedding date and with fatality he accepted its inexorable approach.

On an afternoon in October he was to meet Zoe in Holland Park, by the northern gate. Lisa was going for a fitting of her wedding dress and afterwards to dine with her mother in what he called the medium's lair. So that was all right. He waited by the gate for nearly an hour. When Zoe didn't come, he went to her flat but received no answer to his ring. From his own home he telephoned her five times during the evening, but each time the bell rang into emptiness. He passed a sleepless night, the first night he had been on his own for four months.

All the next day, from work, he kept trying to call her, and for the first time since he had known her he made no call to Lisa. But his own phone was ringing when he got home at six. Of course it was Zoe, it must be. He took up the receiver and heard the fraught voice of Mrs Cleasant.

"Peter?"

Disappointment hurt him like pain. "Yes," he said. "How are you? How's Lisa?"

"Peter, I have very bad news. I think you had better come here. Yes, now. At once."

"What is it? Has anything happened to Lisa?"

"Lisa has—has passed over. Last night she took an over-dose of my pills. I found her dead this morning."

He went out again at once. In the park, at dusk, the leaves were dying and livid, some already fallen. At this point, when they had been showing their first green of spring, he had taken the photograph, at this, he had seated her in a sunny open space and she had seen Zoe.

Mrs Cleasant wasn't alone. Some of the members of her magic circle were with her, but she was calmer than he had ever seen her and he guessed she was drugged.

"How did it happen?" he said.

"I told you. She took an overdose."

"But—why?" He shrank away from the medium's eyes which, staring, seemed to see ghosts behind him.

"Nothing to do with you, Peter," said Mrs Cleasant. "She loved you, you know that. And she was so happy yesterday. Her fitting was cancelled. She said she wanted fresh air because it was such a lovely day, and then she'd walk over to you. She'd thrown away her charm—that amulet she wore— because she said you didn't like it. I told her not to, as it was a harmless thing and might do good. Who knows? If she had been wearing it . . ."

"Ah, if she had been under the Protection!" said the medium.

Mrs Cleasant went on, "We were going out to dinner. I waited and waited for her. When she didn't come I went alone. I thought she was with you, safe with you. But I came back early and there she was, looking so tired and afraid. She said she was going to bed. I asked her if there was anything wrong and she said . . ." But Mrs Cleasant's voice quavered into sobs and the witch women fluttered about her, touching her and murmuring.

It was the medium who explained in her corpse voice. "She said she had seen her own double in the park."

"But that was six months ago," he burst out. "That was in April!"

"No, she saw her own double yesterday afternoon, her image walking in the garden. And she dared to speak to it. Who can tell what your own death will tell you when you dare to address it?"

He ran away from them then, out of the house. He hailed a taxi and in a shaking whisper asked the driver to take him to where Zoe lived. All the lights were on in her windows. He rang the bell, rang it again and again. Then, while the lights still blazed but she didn't come down, he hammered on the door with his fists, calling her name. When he knew she wasn't going to come, that he had lost her and her image, her double and her, forever, he sank down on the doorstep and wept.

The taxi driver, returning along the street in search of a fare, supposed him to be drunk, and learning his address from the broken mutterings, took him home.

Gogol's Wife
Tommaso Landolfi

Tommaso Landolfi

(Italy, 1908-1979)

Tommaso Landolfi was born in Pico, in the province of Frosinone, between Rome and Naples. His first volume of stories, *Dialogo dei massimi sistemi*, appeared in 1937, and was followed by nearly a dozen other books. Although he was considered one of Italy's modern masters, few read him; he did not frequent literary circles and so protected his privacy that, when his collected stories were published in 1961, the jacket flap bore the whimsical notice: "This space is left blank at the request of the author." When the U.S. edition of *Gogol's Wife and Other Stories* appeared, the jacket did show Landolfi, but with face obscured by his outstretched, splay-fingered hand.

Yet Landolfi, who wrote in the tradition of Poe, Gogol, and Kafka, was one of the great fantasists of this century. Susan Sontag compared him with Borges and Isak Dinesen and thought him "a greater writer than either." In his stories we are made to confront fears that we repress in order to sustain a tenuous reality: a man is driven mad by an enigmatic lizard; a poet discovers, to his dismay, that he is writing in a nonexistent language; a man who lusts after a woman's bosom finds, in place of proud nipples, the flaccid flesh of an old man's toothless mouth.

Landolfi translated the work of Nikolai Gogol, a fellow recluse whose real life was no less bizarre than the fantastic premise of "Gogol's Wife": that the great master's "soul's far better half" was not a woman, but a "doll made of thick rubber the hue of flesh."

Gogol's Wife

Thus confronted with the complex question of Nikolai Vasilyevich's wife, I am overwhelmed by hesitation. Do I have any
right to reveal something that nobody knows, something that
my unforgettable friend himself kept hidden from everyone
(and with good reason) and that will undoubtedly serve only
the most evil and foolish interpretations? Not to mention the
many sordid, sanctimonious and hypocritical souls who will
be offended, and perhaps some truly honest souls too, if they
still come that way? Do I have any right, finally, to reveal
something before which my own sensibility shrinks, when I
am not inclined toward a more or less open disapproval? But,
after all, precise duties are incumbent upon me as a biographer: and seeing that each and every piece of news about such
a lofty man might turn out to be precious to us and to future
generations, I would not wish to entrust it to transient judg-
ment, in other words, to conceal something that could only
eventually, if ever, be judged sanely. Because who are we to
condemn? Have we been granted the right to know not only
the needs of these outstanding men, but also the superior and

general ends to which their actions (which we may consider vile) correspond? Certainly not, since fundamentally we understand nothing of such privileged natures. "It's true," a great man said, "I pee too, but for altogether different reasons."

But dispensing with all that, I will come to what I know undeniably, what I know without a shadow of a doubt about the controversial question, which I can prove in any case to be otherwise, at least I dare hope; thus, I will not summarize any of that, since at this point it is superfluous to the current phase of Gogol studies.

Gogol's wife, it must be said, was not a woman, nor was she a human being, nor a living creature of any kind, nor an animal or plant (as some have insinuated); she was simply a doll. Yes, a doll; and this well explains the bewilderment, or worse, the indignation of some biographers, who were also personal friends of our Man, and who complained they had never seen her although they frequented her great husband's house quite often; not only that, they had "never even heard her voice." Hence, goodness knows what dark, disgraceful and perhaps even abominable complications they may have inferred. But no, gentlemen, everything is always simpler than one might believe; you never heard her voice simply because she could not speak. Or more precisely, she could only speak under certain conditions, as we will see, and in all those cases, except one, only to Nikolai Vasilyevich. But let me dispense with useless and facile refutations, and let us work toward the most precise and complete description possible of the being or object in question.

Gogol's so-called wife, then, looked like a common doll made of thick rubber the hue of flesh, or as it is often called, skin color, and was nude regardless of the season. But since women's skin is not always the same color, I should specify that hers was generally somewhat fair and smooth, like that of some brunettes. It, or she, was in fact (but must this be

said?) of the female sex. Indeed, let me add immediately that
she was highly fickle in her characteristics, although ob-
viously, she could not change her sex. Yet without a doubt
she could appear thin, almost flat-chested and straight-hip-
ped, more like an ephebe than a woman, on one occasion,
and on another, exceedingly buxom, or to put it plainly,
plump. She frequently changed her hair color as well as the
other hair on her body, sometimes to match and sometimes
not. Thus she could also alter other minute particulars, such
as the placement of moles, the color of her mucous mem-
branes, and so on; and even to a certain extent, the actual
color of her skin. Therefore, ultimately, one must ask oneself
what she really was, and if he should speak of her as a
singular being; yet, as we shall see, it would not be wise to
insist on this point.

The reasons for these changes were, as my readers must
already have guessed, none other than the very will of Nikolai
Vasilyevich. He would inflate her accordingly, change her
hairstyle and other body fuzz, anoint her with oils and touch
her up in various ways in order to obtain the closest possible
version of the type of woman that suited him that day or that
moment. Indeed, he sometimes amused himself by following
the natural inclination of his fantasy, manipulating her into
grotesque and monstrous forms. Because clearly, beyond a
certain air capacity, she only became deformed, but she would
appear equally hideous if the volume remained too low. But
Gogol soon tired of such experiments, as he considered them
"basically disrespectful" of his wife, whom he loved in his
own way (as inscrutable as it might be to us). He loved her,
but one might ask precisely which of her incarnations he
loved? Alas, I have already indicated that the rest of the
present account might provide some sort of answer. Oh, dear,
how could I have just stated that Nikolai Vasilyevich's will
governed that woman! In a limited sense yes, that is true, but
it is just as certain that she soon became his tyrant rather than

his slave. And this is where the abyss, or if you will, the jaws of Tartarus, open. But let us proceed in an orderly manner.

I also said that Gogol obtained an approximation of the woman that suited him from one occasion to the next. I should also add that in those rare cases when the resulting form completely incarnated his fantasy, Nikolai Vasilyevich fell in love, "in an exclusive manner" (as he put it in his native tongue), which actually created a stable relationship for a certain period, that is, until he fell out of love with her appearance.

I must say that I have only come across three or four instances of such violent passions, or as the unfortunate expression goes today, crushes, in the life, or might I say the married life, of the great writer. Let us add right away for the sake of expedience that several years after his so-called marriage, Gogol even gave his wife a name; it was "Caracas," which, if I'm not mistaken, is the capital of Venezuela. I have never been able to comprehend the reasons for such a choice: the eccentricities of lofty minds!

As for her overall shape, Caracas was what is known as a "beautiful woman," well-built and proportioned in all her parts. As remarked earlier, even the smallest characteristics of her sex were where they should have been. Particularly noteworthy were her genitalia (if this word can have any meaning here), which Gogol allowed me to observe one memorable evening; but more about that later. This was the result of an ingenious folding of the rubber. Nothing had been overlooked: the pressurized air inside her and other clever devices made her easy to use.

Caracas also had a skeleton, though a rudimentary one, made perhaps from whalebone; special care had been taken in the construction of the rib cage, the bones of the pelvis and the cranium. The first two systems were more or less visible, as one would expect, in proportion to the thickness of the so-called adipose tissue which covered it. If I may quickly add, it is a real pity that Gogol never wanted to reveal the identity of the artist behind such a beautiful piece of work; indeed, I never understood the obstinacy of his refusal.

Nikolai Vasilyevich inflated his wife through the anal sphincter with the aid of a pump of his own invention, somewhat similar to those that are held in place by the feet and which are commonly seen in mechanics' garages; in the anus there was a small movable valve, or whatever it is called in technical jargon, comparable to the mitral valve in the heart, such that once the body was inflated it could still take in air without losing any. To deflate it, one had to unscrew a little cap located in the mouth, at the back of the throat. And nevertheless . . . But let's not jump ahead.

And now I think I have covered all of the notable particulars of this being—except to remark upon the stupendous row of little teeth which graced her mouth and her brown eyes which, despite constant immobility, feigned life perfectly. Good Lord, feigned is not the word for it! Indeed, one really cannot say anything legitimately about Caracas. The color of those eyes could also be modified through a rather long and tedious process, yet Gogol rarely did this. And finally I must speak about her voice, which I had occasion to hear only once. But first I must touch upon the relationship between the spouses, and here I can no longer proceed randomly, or answer everything with the same absolute certainty. I could not do that in good conscience, for what I am about to relate is too confusing, inherently and in my own mind. Here nevertheless are my memories, as chaotic as they may be.

The first and indeed the last time I heard Caracas speak was on an intensely intimate evening spent in the room where the woman, if I may be allowed this verb, lived; nobody was permitted to enter. The room was decorated in somewhat of an Oriental style, had no windows and was located in the most impenetrable corner of the house. I had not been unaware that she spoke, but Gogol never wished to clarify the circumstances under which she did. There we were, you see, the two, or three of us. Nikolai Vasilyevich and I were drinking vodka and discussing Butkov's novel; I remember that he digressed from the topic a bit and was insisting on the need for radical reforms in the inheritance laws; we had nearly forgotten her. And then in a hoarse, meek voice like Venus in the nuptial bed, she said point-blank, "I have to go poop." I gave a start, thinking I had misheard, and I looked at her: she was sitting propped against a wall on a pile of pillows, and on that day she was a soft, gorgeous blonde, and rather fleshy. Her face seemed to have taken on an expression bordering on maliciousness and cunning, childishness and scorn. As for Gogol, he blushed violently and leaped onto her, thrusting two fingers down her throat; and as she began to get thinner and, one might say, paler, she took on that look of astonishment and befuddlement that was truly hers; and at last she shrunk to nothing more than a flabby skin covering a makeshift framework of bones. In fact, since she had an extremely flexible spine (one can intuit how this made for more comfortable use), she nearly folded in half; and she continued to stare at us for the rest of the evening from that degrading position on the floor where she had slid.

"She is either being nasty or joking," Gogol muttered, "because she doesn't suffer such needs." He generally made a show of treating her with disdain in the presence of others, or at least with me.

We continued drinking and conversing, but Nikolai Vasilyevich seemed deeply disturbed and somehow removed. Suddenly he broke off, and taking my hands in his own, burst into tears. "Now what," he exclaimed. "Don't you see, Foma Paskalovic, I loved her!" It must be mentioned that, short of a miracle, none of the forms Caracas took was reproducible; she was a new creation each time, and any attempt to recreate the particular proportions, the particular fullness and so on, of a deflated Caracas would have been in vain. Therefore, that

particular plump blonde was now hopelessly lost to Gogol.
And indeed, this was the pitiful end of one of Nikolai Vasilyevich's few loves which I made a reference to earlier. He
refused to provide any explanation, he refused my consolation, and we parted early that evening. But he had opened his
heart to me in that outburst; from then on he was never as
reticent, and soon he kept no secrets from me. This, parenthe-
tically, was a source of infinite pride.

Things seemed to have gone well for the "couple" during
the first phase of their life together. Nikolai Vasilyevich appeared to be content with Caracas and slept in the same bed
with her regularly. He continued to do this up until the end
as well, admitting with a timid smile that there could not be
a quieter or less tiresome companion than she; nevertheless, I
soon had reason to doubt this, judging mostly from the state
I sometimes found him in when he awoke. Within several
years, however, their relationship became strangely troubled.

This, let me caution once and for all, is merely a schematic
attempt at explanation. But it seems that around that time
the woman began to show an inclination for independence,
or should I say, autonomy. Nikolai Vasilyevich had the bizarre impression that she was assuming a personality of her
own, which, although indecipherable, was distinct from his
own, and she seemed to be slipping, if you will, from his
grasp. It is true that a continuity was finally established
among all her diverse and varied appearances: there was
something in common among all those brunette, blond, au-
burn and red-haired women, among the fat, thin, withered,
pallid and ambered ones. In the beginning of this chapter, I
threw some doubt on the legitimacy of considering Caracas a
single personality; nevertheless, whenever I saw her I could
not free myself of the impression that, incredible as it may
seem, she was essentially one and the same woman. And
perhaps it was precisely this which prompted Gogol to give
her a name.

It is another thing again to try to establish the nature of the quality common to all those forms. Perhaps it was no more and no less than the breath of her creator, Nikolai Vasilye-vich. But truly, it would have been too peculiar for him to be so detached from himself, so conflicted. Because it must be said immediately that whoever Caracas was, she was nonetheless a disturbing presence, and let this be clear, a hostile one. In conclusion, however, neither Gogol nor I ever managed to formulate a vaguely plausible hypothesis concerning her nature. I mean to "formulate" one in rational terms that would be accessible to everyone. I cannot, in any case, suppress an extraordinary incident which occurred during this period.

Caracas fell ill with a shameful disease, or at least Gogol did, although he had never had any contact with other women. I will not even try to speculate on how such a thing happened or from whence the foul illness sprung: I only know that it happened. And that my great unhappy friend sometimes said to me, "So you see, Foma Paskalovic, what was in Caracas' heart: the spirit of syphilis!" But at other times, he blamed himself quite absurdly (he had always had a tendency for self-accusation). This incident was truly catastrophic for the relations between the spouses, which were already confused enough, and for Nikolai Vasilyevich's conflicting feelings. He was thus obliged to undergo continuous and painful cures (as they were in those days). And the situation was aggravated by the fact that in the woman's case, the disease did not initially appear to be curable. I should also add that for some time Gogol continued to pretend that by inflating and deflating his wife and giving her a great variety of appearances, he could create a woman immune to the infection; however, as his efforts were not successful, he had to cease.

But I will shorten the story so as not to bore my readers. Besides, my conclusions are only becoming more and more confused and uncertain. Thus I will hasten toward the tragic denouement. Let it be clear, I must insist upon my view of this: indeed, I was an eyewitness. Would that I had not been!

The years passed. Nikolai Vasilyevich's disgust for his wife grew more intense even though there was no sign that his love for her was diminishing. Toward the end, aversion and attachment put up such a fierce battle in his spirit that he came out of it exhausted and ravaged. His restless eyes, which normally reflected a myriad of expressions and often spoke sweetly to the heart, now nearly always shone with a weak light, as though he were under the effects of a drug. He developed the strangest manias accompanied by the darkest fears. More and more frequently he talked to me of Caracas, accusing her of unlikely and astonishing things. I could not follow him in this, given my occasional dealings with his wife, and the fact that I had little or no intimacy with her; and above all given my sensibility (which is extremely narrow in comparison to his). I will therefore limit my references to some of those accusations without bringing in any of my own personal impressions.

"You understand, don't you, Foma Paskalovic," he often said to me, for example, "you understand that *she's getting old?*" And, caught between unspeakable emotions, he took my hands in his, as was his manner. He also accused Caracas of abandoning herself to her own solitary pleasures although he had explicitly forbidden it. He even began to accuse her of betrayal. But his discussions on this subject ultimately became so obscure that I will refrain from reporting any others.

What appeared certain is that toward the end, Caracas, old or not, was reduced to a bitter, argumentative and hypocritical creature who was subject to religious obsessions. I don't rule out that she may have influenced Gogol's moral attitude during the latter part of his life, an attitude known to all. In any case, the tragedy befell Nikolai Vasilyevich unexpectedly one evening while he was celebrating his silver anniversary with me—unfortunately one of the last nights that we spent together. Exactly what had brought it on just then, when he already seemed resigned to tolerating just about anything from his consort, I cannot, nor is it my place to, say. I do not know what new occurrence may have come about in those days. I am sticking to the facts here; my readers must form their own opinions.

Nikolai Vasilyevich was particularly agitated that evening. His disgust for Caracas seemed to have reached an unprecedented pitch. He had already carried out his famous "vanity burning," that is the burning of his precious manuscripts—I dare not say whether or not at his wife's instigation. He was in an agitated state of mind for other reasons too. As for his physical condition, it grew more pitiful by the day, reinforcing my impression that he might be drugged. Nevertheless, he began to speak rather normally of Belinskij, whose attacks and criticism of the *Correspondence* were causing him concern. But then he broke off suddenly, crying out, "No, no! It's too much, too much. . . . I can't stand it anymore. . . !" as tears streamed from his eyes. And he added other obscure and disconnected exclamations which he failed to clarify. He seemed to be speaking to himself. He clapped his hands together, he shook his head, and after having taken four or five faltering steps, he leaped up only to sit back down.

When Caracas appeared, or more precisely, when we moved to her Oriental room late that night, he began to behave like an old senile man (if I may make such a comparison) whose fixations have gotten the better of him. For example, he kept elbowing me, winking and repeating nonsensically, "Look, there she is, there she is, Foma Paskalovic! . . ." Meanwhile she seemed to be watching him with scornful attention. But behind these "mannerisms," one could sense genuine repulsion, which I suppose had surpassed tolerable limits. In fact . . .

After a time, Nikolai Vasilyevich seemed to pull himself

together. He burst into tears again, but I would almost call
these more manly tears. Once again, he wrung his hands,
grabbed hold of mine and walked up and down muttering:
"No, no more, it's impossible! ... How could I ... such a
thing? ... Such a thing ... to me? How can I possibly bear
this, endure *this*. . . !" and so on. Then, as if he had just then
remembered the pump, he leaped on it suddenly and made
for Caracas in a whirl. Inserting the tube in her anus, he
began to inflate her. Meanwhile he wept and shouted, as if
possessed: "How I love her, my God, how I love her, the poor
dear. . . ! But I must blow her up, wretched Caracas, God's
miserable creature! She must die," alternating these phrases
endlessly.

Caracas was swelling. Nikolai Vasilyevich perspired and
wept as he continued to pump. I wanted to restrain him, but
I didn't have the courage, I don't know why. She began to
look deformed, and soon she took on a monstrous appearance; yet up until then she hadn't showed any sign of alarm,
being used to such pranks. But when she began to feel un-
bearably full, or perhaps when she realized Nikolai Vasilyevich's intentions, she assumed an expression which I can
only describe as stupid and befuddled, and even imploring.
But she never lost that scornful look of hers; though she was
afraid and nearly begging, she still did not believe, could not
believe, the fate that lay ahead for her, could not believe that
her husband could be so audacious. Moreover, he could not
see her because he was standing behind her; I watched her
fascinated, not moving a finger. Finally, the excessive inter-
nal pressure forced out the fragile bones of her cranium,
bringing an indescribable grimace to her face. Her belly,
thighs, hips, breasts, and what I could see of her behind had
reached unimaginable proportions. Then suddenly she bel-
ched and let out a long whistling moan, both phenomena
that could be explained, if you will, by the increasing air
pressure which had suddenly burst open the valve in her

throat. And finally, her eyes bulged out, threatening to pop
out of their sockets. Her ribs were spread so wide that they
had detached from her sternum, and she now looked like a
python digesting a mule. What am I saying? Like an ox, an
elephant! Her genitals, those pink and velvety organs so dear
to Nikolai Vasilyevich, protruded horrendously. At this
point, I deemed her already dead. But Nikolai Vasilyevich,
sweating and weeping, murmured, "My dear, my saint, my
good lady," and continued to pump.

She exploded suddenly, and all at once: thus, it wasn't one
area of her skin that gave out, but her whole surface simultaneously. And she was strewn through the air. The pieces
then drifted back down at varying speeds depending on their
size, which were very small in any case. I distinctly remember
a part of the cheek, with a bit of mouth, dangling from the
corner of the fireplace; and elsewhere, a tatter of breast with
the nipple. Nikolai Vasilyevich was staring at me absent-
mindedly. Then he roused himself, and possessed by a new
mania, went about the task of carefully collecting all those
pitiful little scraps that had once been the smooth skin of
Caracas, all of her. "Good-bye, Caracas," I thought I heard
him murmur, "good-bye, you were too pitiful . . ." And then
he added quickly, distinctly, "Into the fire, into the fire, she
too must burn!" and he crossed himself, with his left hand,
naturally. Once he had gathered up all those withered shreds,
even climbing onto all the furniture so as not to miss any, he
threw them straight into the flames in the fireplace, where
they began to burn slowly with an exceedingly unpleasant
odor. Indeed, Nikolai Vasilyevich, like all Russians, had a
passion for throwing important things into the fire.

Red in the face, wearing an expression of unspeakable
desperation and sinister triumph, he contemplated the pyre
of those miserable remains; he grabbed my arm and clutched
it violently. But once those shredded spoils had begun to
burn, he seemed to rouse himself once again, as if suddenly

remembering something or making a momentous decision; then abruptly, he ran out of the room. A few moments later, I heard his broken, strident voice addressing me through the door. "Foma Paskolovic," he shouted, "Foma Paskolovic, promise me you won't look, *golubcik*, at what I'm about to do!" I don't remember clearly what I said, or whether I tried somehow to calm him. But he insisted: I had to promise him, as if he were a child, that I would stand with my face to the wall and wait for his permission to turn around. Then the door clattered open and Nikolai Vasilyevich rushed headlong into the room and ran toward the fireplace.

Here I must confess my weakness, though it was justified, considering the extraordinary circumstances in which I found myself: I turned around before Nikolai Vasilyevich told me to. The impulse was stronger than me. I turned just in time to notice that he was carrying something in his arms, something he hurled into the flames, which then flared. In any case, the yearning to see which had irresistibly taken hold of me, conquering every other impulse, now impelled me toward the fireplace. But Nikolai Vasilyevich stepped in front of me and butted his chest against me with a force I did not believe him capable of. Meanwhile, the object burned, giving off great fumes. By the time he began to calm down, all I could make out was a heap of silent ashes.

Truthfully, if I wanted to see, it was mainly because I had already glimpsed, but only glimpsed. Perhaps I best not report anything else, or introduce any element of uncertainty in this veracious narration. And yet, an eyewitness account is not complete if the witness does not also relate what he thinks, even if he is not completely certain of it. In short, that something was a child. Not a child of flesh and blood, of course, but something like a puppet or a boy doll made of rubber. Something that, in a word, could be called Caracas' son. Could I have been delirious too? That I cannot say; yet this is what I saw, however confusedly, with my own eyes.

But what sentiment was I obeying just now, when I refrained from saying that as Nikolai Vasilyevich entered the room, he was muttering, "Him too, him too!"

And now I have exhausted all that I know of Nikolai Vasilyevich's wife. I will relate what became of him in the next chapter, the last chapter of his life. But any interpretation of his relationship and his feelings for his wife, as for all others, is another matter altogether and a good deal more problematical. Nevertheless, I attempt that in another section of the present volume and refer the reader to it. In any case, I hope that I have cast sufficient light on this controversial question, and that even if I have not laid bare the mystery of Gogol, I have clarified the mystery of his wife. I have implicitly refuted the nonsensical accusation that he ever maltreated or beat his companion, and all the other absurdities. And fundamentally, what other intention should a humble biographer like myself have if not to serve the memory of the lofty man who is the object of his study?

Translated from the Italian by Kathrine Jason

August 25, 1983

Jorge Luis Borges

Jorge Luis Borges

(Argentina, 1899-1986)

If Jorge Luis Borges had not lived, someone would surely have dreamt him. There is a strong feeling of *déjà vu* on first reading Borges's fables and stories, what Colin Wilson called "a kind of nostalgia for the infinite." Like Borges's own creation Pierre Menard, who rewrites Cervantes's *Don Quixote*, Borges read, admired and rewrote, or dreamed variations upon the work of, among others, Poe, Chesterton, Wilde, Hawthorne, Kipling, and Beckford. He himself noted, "My 'Dr Brodie's Report' is taken from Swift and 'Death and the Compass' is like Conan Doyle in 3-D."

Borges numbered the double—along with time travel, the contamination of reality by dream, and the work within a work—among the four basic devices of fantastic literature. In "Three Versions of Judas," he suggests that Judas reflects Christ, that Christ was Judas, or perhaps the reverse. The parable "Borges and I" begins, "The other one, the one called Borges, is the one things happen to," and concludes, "I do not know which of us has written this page." In "August 25, 1983," Borges finally meets that *alter ego*.

August 25, 1983

I saw by the little station clock that it was a few minutes past
eleven at night. I walked to the hotel. I felt, as on so many
other occasions, the relief and resignation inspired by places
we know well. The heavy gate was open; the house stood in
darkness.

I entered the hall where dim mirrors duplicated the potted
plants in the room. Strangely enough, the hotel-keeper didn't
recognize me and handed me the register. I took the pen
which was chained to the desk, dipped it in the bronze
inkwell and, as I bent over the open book, there occurred the
first of the many surprises which that night was to offer me.
My name, Jorge Luis Borges, had already been written on the
page and the ink was still fresh.

The hotel-keeper said, "I thought you'd already gone upstairs." Then he peered at me more closely and corrected
himself. "I'm sorry, sir, the other looks a lot like you. But
you're younger of course."

"What room is he in?"

"He asked for number nineteen," was the answer. It was as
I feared.

I dropped the pen and ran up the stairs. Room nineteen was on the second floor and looked on to a poor and badly tended courtyard with a veranda and, I seem to remember, a bench. It was the highest room in the hotel. I tried the handle and the door opened. The lamp had not been switched off. Under the harsh light I recognized myself. There I was, lying on my back on the small iron bed, older, wizened and very pale, the eyes lost on the high stucco mouldings. The voice reached me. It wasn't exactly mine; it was like the voice I often hear in my recordings, unpleasant and monotonous.

"How strange," it said. "We are two and we are one. But then, there is nothing really strange in dreams."

I asked bewildered, "Is all this a dream?"

"It is certainly my last dream."

He pointed at the empty bottle on the marble top of the night-table.

"But you have still got plenty to dream before reaching this night. What date is it for you?"

"I don't know exactly," I answered uncertainly. "But yesterday was my sixty-first birthday."

"When you reach this night, your eighty-fourth birthday will have been yesterday. Today is August 25, 1983."

"So many more years to wait," I said in a low voice.

"I have nothing left," he said suddenly. "I can die any day now. I can fade into that which I don't know and yet keep on dreaming of the double. That hackneyed theme given to me by Stevenson and mirrors!"

I felt that to mention Stevenson was a last farewell, not a pedantic allusion. I was he, and I understood. Even the most dramatic moments are not enough to turn one into Shakespeare and coin memorable phrases.

To change the subject I said, "I knew what would happen to you. In this very place, in one of the lower rooms, we began to draft the story of this suicide."

"Yes," he answered slowly, as if collecting vague

memories, "but I don't see the resemblance. In that draft I bought a one-way ticket to Adrogué, and in the Hotel Las Delicias I climbed to room nineteen, the farthest room of all. There I committed suicide."

"That is why I am here," I said to him.

"Here? But we are always here. Here I am dreaming of you, in the apartment of Calle Maipú. Here I am dying in the room that used to be mother's."

"That used to be mother's," I repeated, trying not to understand. "And I am dreaming of you in room nineteen, on the top floor."

"Who is dreaming whom? I know I am dreaming you but I don't know whether you are dreaming me. The hotel in Adrogué was pulled down many years ago—twenty, maybe thirty. Who knows!"

"I am the dreamer," I answered with a certain defiance.

"But don't you see that the important thing is to discover whether there is only one dreamer or two?"

"I am Borges who has seen your name in the register and has climbed up to this room."

"Borges am I, dying in Calle Maipú."

There was a moment of silence. Then the other said, "Let's put ourselves to the test. Which was the most terrible moment of our life?"

I leant over towards him and we both spoke at the same time. I know we both lied. A faint smile lit the old face. I felt that the smile somehow reflected my own.

"We have lied to each other," he said, "because we feel two and not one. The truth is that we are two and we are one."

The conversation was beginning to irritate me. I told him so. And I added, "And you, in 1983, won't you reveal something of the years that lie before me?"

"What can I tell you, my poor Borges? The misfortunes to which you have grown accustomed will keep on happening. You will live alone in this house. You will touch the letterless books and the Swedenborg medallion and the wooden box with the Federal Cross. Blindness isn't darkness—it's a form of loneliness. You will return to Iceland."

"Iceland! Iceland of the seas!"

"In Rome you will say a few lines by Keats whose name, like that of all other men, was written on water."

"I have never been to Rome."

"There are other things as well. You will write our best poem, and it will be an elegy."

"To the death of . . ." I said. I did not dare utter the name.

"No. She will live longer than you." We sat in silence. Then he continued.

"You will write that book we dreamt of for so long. Towards 1979 you will understand that your so-called works are nothing but a series of sketches, miscellaneous drafts, and you will yield to the vain and superstitious temptation of writing your one great book. The superstition that has inflicted upon us Goethe's *Faust, Salammbô, Ulysses*. To my amazement, I have filled too many pages."

"And in the end you realized you had failed."

"Something worse. I realized it was a masterpiece in the most oppressive sense of the word. My good intentions did not go farther than the first few pages. In the others lay the labyrinths, the knives, the man who believes he is a dream, the reflection that believes itself to be real, the tigers of night, the battles turned to blood, Juan Muraña fatal and blind, Macedonio's voice, the ship made of the fingernails of the dead, old English spoken through so many days."

"I know that museum well," I observed, not without irony.

"And then false memories too, the double play of symbols, the long enumerations, the craft of good prose, the imperfect symmetries that the critics discover with glee, the not always apocryphal quotations."

"Have you published this book?"

"I toyed—without conviction—with the melodramatic idea of destroying it, perhaps with fire. I finally published it in Madrid under another name. It was described as the work of a vulgar imitator of Borges who had the disadvantage of not being Borges and of having repeated the superficial features of the model."

"I'm not surprised," I said. "Every writer ends by being his own least intelligent disciple."

"That book was one of the roads that led me to this night. As to the others, the humiliation of old age, the certainty of having already lived all those days to come . . ."

"I won't write that book," I said.

"Yes you will. My words, which now are the present, will be barely the memory of a dream."

His dogmatic tone, no doubt the same one I use in the classroom, annoyed me. I was bothered by the fact that we resembled each other so much, and that he should take advantage of the impunity given him by the nearness of death. In revenge I asked him: "Are you really so certain you are about to die?"

"Yes," he answered. "I feel a sort of sweet peacefulness and relief which I have never felt before. I cannot explain it to you. All words require a shared experience. Why do you seem annoyed by what I'm telling you?"

"Because we are far too alike. I hate your face which is a caricature of mine. I hate your voice which apes my own. I hate your pathetic way of building sentences, which is mine."

"So do I," said the other. "That is why I have decided to kill myself."

A bird sang in the street.

"The last one," said the other.

With a gesture he called me to his side. His hand took hold of mine. I drew back, fearing that both hands would fade into one. He said:

"The stoics have taught us not to regret leaving this life: the gates of prison are at last open. I have always thought of life in this way, but my sloth and cowardice made me hesitate. Some twelve days ago I gave a conference in La Plata on the sixth book of the *Aeneid*. Suddenly, repeating an hexameter, I knew which was the road to take, and I made up my mind. From that moment onward I felt invulnerable. My fate will be yours, you will receive this sudden revelation in the midst of Virgil's Latin, and you will have forgotten this curious and prophetic dialogue which takes place in two places and two moments in time. When you dream it again you will be the one I am now and I will be your dream."

"I won't forget it and tomorrow I'll write it down."

"It will lie deep inside your memory, beneath the tide of dreams. When you write it, you will believe you are inventing a fantastic story. But it won't be tomorrow. You still have several years to wait."

He stopped talking; I realized he was dead. In a certain sense I died with him. Anxiously I leant forward over the top of the pillow but there was no one there.

I fled from the room. Outside there was no courtyard, no marble staircase, no large silent hotel, no eucalyptus, no statues, no arches, no fountains, no gate of a country house in Adrogué.

Outside were other dreams, waiting for me.

Translated from the Spanish by Alberto Manguel

Petition

John Barth

John Barth

(United States, b. 1930)

John Barth has written, "My books tend to come in pairs; my sentences in twin members." Born a fraternal twin, his novels (*The Sot-Weed Factor, Giles Goat-Boy, The End of the Road, Chimera*) exhibit a fascination with twins, doubles, word play and the nature of self.

In the *New York Times Book Review* ("The Making of a Writer," May 9, 1982) John Barth described his experience of being a twin: "Twins of any sort share the curious experience of accommodating ... a peer companion from the beginning, even in the womb; of entering the world with an established sidekick, rather than alone, of acquiring speech and the other basic skills à deux, in the meanwhile sharing a language before speech and beyond speech. Speech, baby twins may feel, is for the Others.... I have sometimes felt that a twin who happens to be a writer ... might take this 'shtik' by the other end and use schizophrenia, say, as an image for what he knows to be his literal case: that he once was more than one person and somehow now is less."

In the past there have been numerous examples of Siamese twins, many of whom have achieved great popularity on the stage and in circuses and who, though burdened by their strangeness, yet lived with dignity and courage. "Petition," in which a Siamese twin argues for separation from his gross and lecherous other-self, is perhaps Barth's paramount handling of the twin motif.

Petition

April 21, 1931

His Most Gracious Majesty Prajadhipok, Descendant
   of Buddha, King of North and South, Supreme Arbiter of
   the Ebb and Flow of the Tide, Brother of the Moon, Half-
   Brother of the Sun, Possessor of the Four-and-Twenty Golden Umbrellas
Ophir Hall
White Plains, New York

Sir:
   Welcome to America. An ordinary citizen extends his wish
that your visit with us be pleasant, your surgery successful.
   Though not myself a native of your kingdom, I am and
have been most alive to its existence and concerns—unlike the
average American, alas, to whose imagination the name of
that ancient realm summons only white elephants and blue-
eyed cats. I am aware, for example, that it was Queen Ram-
bai's father's joke that he'd been inside the Statue of Liberty

but never in the United States, having toured the Paris
foundry while that symbol was a-casting; in like manner I
may say that I have dwelt in a figurative Bangkok all my life.
My brother, with whose presumption and other faults I hope
further to acquaint you in the course of this petition, has even
claimed (in his cups) descent from the mad King Phaya Takh
Sin, whose well-deserved assassination—like the surgical ex-
cision of a cataract, if I may be so bold—gave to a benighted
land the luminous dynasty of Chakkri, whereof Your Majesty
is the latest and brightest son. Here as elsewhere my brother
lies or is mistaken: we are Occidental, for better or worse, and
while our condition is freakish, our origin is almost certainly
commonplace. Yet though my brother's claim is false and
(should he press it upon you, as he might) in contemptible
taste, it may serve the purpose of introducing to you his
character, my wretched situation, and my petition to your
magnanimity.

The reign of the Chakkris began in violence and threatens
to end in blindness; my own history commences with a kind
of blindness and threatens to terminate in murder. Happily,
our American surgeons are equal to the former threat; my
prayer is that Your Majesty—reciprocally, as it were—may
find it in his heart to address himself to the latter. The press
reports your pledge to liberate three thousand inmates of your
country's prisons by April next, to celebrate both the restora-
tion of your eyesight and the sesquicentennial of your dynasty: a regal gesture. But there are prisoners and prisoners;
my hope is for another kind of release, from what may not
unfairly be termed life-imprisonment for no crime whatever,
only the misfortune of being born my brother's brother. That
the prerogative of kings yet retains, even in the New World,
some trace of its old divinity, is amply proved by President
Hoover's solicitude for your comfort and all my countrymen's eagerness to serve you. The magazines proclaim the

triflingest details of your daily round; society talks of nothing
else but your comings and goings; a word from you sends
government officers scurrying, reroutes express-trains, stops
presses, marshals the finest medical talents in the nation.
Give commands, then, that I be liberated at long last from a
misery absolute as your monarchy!

Will you counsel resignation to my estate, even affirmation
of it? Will you cite the example of Chang and Eng, whom
your ancestor thought to put to death and ended by blessing?
But Chang and Eng were different from my brother and me,
because so much the same; Change and Eng were as the left
hand to the right; Chang and Eng were bound heart to heart:
their common navel, which to prick was to injure both, was
an emblem of their fraternity, as was the manner of their
sitting, each with an arm about the other's shoulders. Haven't
I wept with envy of sturdy Chang, loyal Eng? Haven't I
invoked them, vainly, as exemplars not only of moral grace
but of practical efficiency? Their introduction of the "double
chop" for cutting logs, a method still employed by pairs of
Carolina woodsmen; their singular skill at driving four-horse
teams down the lumber trails of their adopted state; their
good-humored baiting of railway conductors, to whom they
would present a single ticket, acknowledging that one might
be put off the train, but insisting on the other's right to
transportation; their resourceful employment of the same
reasoning on the occasion of one's arrest, when the other
loyally threatened to sue if he too were jailed; their happy
marriage to a pair of sisters, who bore them twenty-two
healthy children in their separate households; their alterna-
tion of authority and residence every three days, rain or shine,
each man master under his own roof—a schedule followed
faithfully until Chang's death at sixty-three; Eng's touching
last request, as he himself expired of sympathy and terror
three hours later, that his brother's dead body be moved even

closer—didn't I recite these marvels like a litany to *my* brother in the years when I still could hope we might get along?

Yet it may surprise you to learn that even Chang and Eng, those paragons of cooperation, had their differences. Chang was a tippler, Eng a teetotaller; Eng liked all-night checker games, Chang was no gambler; in at least one election they cast their votes for opposing candidates; the arrest aforementioned, though it came to nothing, was for the crime of assault—committed by one against the other. Especially following marriage their differences increased, and if upon returning to the exhibition stage (after the Civil War) they made a show of unanimity, it was to raise money in the hope that some surgeon could part them at last. All this, mind, between veritable Heavenly Twins, sons of the mystical East, whose religions and philosophies—no criticism intended— have ever minimized distinctions, denying even the difference between Sameness and Difference. How altogether contrary is the case of my brother and me! (*He*, as might be expected, denies that the cases are different, contradicts this denial by denying at the same time that we are two in the first place— and would no doubt deny the contradiction as well, with equal obstinacy, should Your Majesty point it out to him.) Only consider: whereas Chang and Eng were bound breast to breast by a good long band that allowed them to walk, sit, and sleep side by side, my brother and I are fastened front to rear—my belly to the small of his back—by a leash of flesh heartbreakingly short. In consequence he never lays eyes on the wretch he forever drags about—no wonder he denies me, agrees with the doctors that such a union is impossible, and claims my utterance and inspiration for his own!—while I see nothing else the day long (unless over his shoulder) but his stupid neck-nape, which I know better than my name. He obscures my view, sits in my lap (never mind how his weight impedes my circulation), smothers me in his wraps. What I suffer in the bathroom is too disgusting for Your Majesty's ears. By night it's scramble or be crushed when he tosses in our bed, pitching and snoring so in his dreams that my own are nightmares; by day I must match his stride like the hinder half of a vaudeville horse until, exhausted, I clamber on him pick-a-back. Small comfort that I may outlast him, despite his greater strength, by riding him thus; when he goes I go, Eng after Chang, and in the meanwhile I must go *where* he goes as well, and suffer his insults along the way. No matter to him that in one breath he denies my existence, in the next affirms it with his oaths and curses: I am Anchises to his Aeneas, he will have it; Old Man of the Sea to his Sinbad; I am his cross, his albatross; I, lifelong victim of his beastliness, he calls the monkey on his back!

No misery, of course, but has its little compensations, however hollow or theoretical. What couldn't we accomplish if he'd cooperate, with me as his back-up man! Only let me count cadence and him go more regularly, there'd be no stumbling; I could prod, tickle, goose him into action if he'd not ignore me; I'd be the eyes in the back of his head, his unobserved prompter and mentor. Cloaked in the legal immunity of Chang-Eng's gambit we could do what we pleased, be wealthy in no time. Even within the law we'd have the world for our oyster, our capacity twice any rival's. Strangers to loneliness, we could make rich our leisure hours: bicycle in tandem, sing close harmony, play astonishing piano, read Plato aloud, assemble mahjongg tiles in half the time. I'd be no prude were we as close in temperament as in body; we could make any open-minded woman happy beyond her most amorous reveries—or, lacking women, delight each other in ways that Chang and Eng could never. . . .

Vain dreams; we are nothing alike. I am slight, my brother is gross. He's incoherent but vocal; I'm articulate and mute. He's ignorant but full of guile; I think I may call myself reasonably educated, and if ingenuous, no more so I hope

than the run of scholars. My brother is gregarious: he deals
with the public; earns and spends our income; tends (but
slovenly) the house and grounds; makes, entertains, and loses
friends; indulges in hobbies; pursues ambitions and women.
For my part, I am by nature withdrawn, even solitary: an
observer of life, a meditator, a taker of notes, a dreamer if you
will—yet not a brooder; it's he who moods and broods, today
hilarious, tomorrow despondent; I myself am stoical, detached as it were—of necessity, or I'd have long since perished
of despair. More to the point, what intelligence my brother
has is inclined to synthesis, mine to analysis; he denies that
we are two, yet refuses to compromise and cooperate; I affirm
our difference—all the difference in the world!—but have
endeavored in vain to work out with him a reasonable coha-
bitation. Untutored and clumsy, he will nevertheless make
flatulent noises upon the trombone, write ungainly verses,
dance awkwardly with women, hold grunting conversations,
jerrybuild a roof over our heads; I, whose imagination en-
compasses Aristotle, Shakespeare, Bach—I'd never so pre-
sume; yet let me point out to him, however diplomatically,
however constructively, the shortcomings of his efforts beside
genuine creation: he flies into a rage, shreds his doggerel,
dents his horn, quarrels with his "sweetheart" (who perhaps
was laughing at him all along), abandons carpentry, beats his
chest in heroical self-pity, or sulks in a corner for days together. I don't even mention his filthy personal habits: what
consolation that he swipes his bum and occasionally soaps
his stinking body? Only the sinner needs absolution, and one
sin breeds another: because I ride on his back and am content
to nourish myself with infrequent sips of tea, I neither per-
spire nor defecate, but merely emit a discreet vapor, of neutral
scent, and tiny puffs of what could pass for talc. Other sustenance I draw less from our common bond, as he might claim,
than from books, from introspection, most of all from revery
and fancy, without which I'd soon enough starve. But he, he

eats anything, lusts after anything, goes to any length to make me wretched. His very excrements he will sniff and savor; he belches up gases, farts in my lap; not content that I must ride atop him, as on a rutting stallion, while he humps his whores, he will torment me in the shower-bath by bending over to draw me against him and pinching at me with his hairy cheeks. Yet let me flinch away, or in a frenzy of disgust attempt to rupture our bond though it kill us (as I sometimes strained to do in years gone by): he turns my revulsion into horrid sport, runs out and snaps back like a paddle-ball or plays crack-the-whip at every turn in our road. Why go on? We have nothing in common but the womb that bore, the flesh that shackles, the grave that must soon receive us. If my situation has any advantage it's only that I can see him without his seeing me; can therefore study and examine our bond, how ever to dissolve it, and take certain surreptitious measures to that end, such as writing this petition. Futile perhaps; desperate certainly. The alternative is madness.

All very well, you may say: lamentable as our situation is, it's nothing new; we were born this way and have somehow muddled through thirty-five years; not even a king has his own way in everything; in the matter of congenital endowment it's potluck for all of us, we must grin and bear it, the weakest to the wall, et cetera. God knows I am no whiner; I've broken heart and spirit to make the best of a bad hand of cards; at the slimmest hint of sympathy from my brother, the least suggestion of real fraternity, I melt with gratitude, must clamber aboard lest I swoon of joy; my tears run in his hair and down the courses of his face, one would think it was he who wept. And were it simply a matter of accumulated misery, or the mere happenstance of your visit, I'd not burden you (and my own sensibility) with this complaint. What prompts my plea is the coincidence of your arrival and a critical turn in our history and situation.

I pass over the details of our past, a tiresome chronicle.

Some say our mother died a-bearing us, others that she perished of dismay soon after; just as possibly, she merely put us out. The man we called Father exhibited us throughout our childhood, but the age was more hardened to monstrosity than Chang's and Eng's; we never prospered; indeed we were scarcely noticed. In earliest babyhood I didn't realize I was two; it was the intractability of that creature always before me —going left when I would go right, bawling for food when I would sleep, laughing when I wept—that opened my eyes to the possibility he was other than myself; the teasing of playmates, who mocked our contretemps, verified that suspicion, and I began my painful schooling in detachment. Early on I proposed to my brother a judicious alliance (with myself, naturally, as director of our activities and final arbiter of our differences, he being utterly a creature of impulse); he would none of my proposal. Through childhood our antipathies merely smoldered, as we both submitted perforce, however grudgingly, to Father (who at least never denied our twoness, which, to be sure, was his livelihood); it was upon our fleeing his government, in adolescence, that they flamed. My attempt to direct our partnership ended in my brother's denying first my efficacy, then my authority, finally my reality. He pretended to believe, offstage as well as on, that the audience's interest was in him as a solo performer and not in the pair of us as a freak; hidden from the general view, unable to speak except in whispers, I could take only feeblest revenge: I would wave now and then between the lines of his stupid performances, grimace behind his back and over his shoulder, make signs to mock or contradict his asseverations. Let him deny me, he couldn't ignore me; I tripped him up, confused, confounded him, and though in the end he usually prevailed, I pulled against him every step of his way, spoiled his pleasure, halved his force, and on more than one occasion stalled him entirely.

The consequent fiascos, the rages and rampages of his

desperation, are too dreadful to recount; them too I pass over, with a shudder. For some time now our connection has been an exasperated truce punctuated with bitter bursts of hostility, as between old mismatched spouses or weary combatants; the open confrontations are less frequent because more vicious, the interim resentments more deep because more resigned. Each new set-to, legatee of all its predecessors, is more destructive than the last; at the merest popgun-pop, artillery bristles. However radically, therefore, our opposition restricts our freedom, we each had come to feel, I believe, that the next real violence between us would be the last, fatal to one and thus to both, and so were more or less resigned to languishing, disgruntled, in our impasse, for want of alternatives. Then between us came Thalia, love, the present crisis.

It will scarcely surprise you that we arrived late at sexuality. Ordinary girls fled from our advances, or cruelly mocked us; had our bookings not fetched us to the capitals of Europe, whose liberal ladies sought us out for novelty's sake, we'd kept our chastity perforce till affluent maturity, for common prostitutes raised their fees, at sight of us, beyond our adolescent means. Even so, it was my brother did all the clipping, I being out of reach except to surrogate gratifications; only when a producer of unusual motion pictures in Berlin, with the resourcefulness characteristic of his nation, discovered Thalia and brought her to us, did I know directly the experience of coition. I did not enjoy it.

More accurately, I was rent by emotions as at odds as I and my brother. Thalia—a pretty young contortionist of good family obliged by the misery of the times to prostitute her art in exotic nightclubs and films—I admired tremendously, not alone for her merry temper and the talent wherewith she achieved our connection, but for her silent forbearance, not unlike my own, in the face as it were of my brother's abuse. But how expect me to share the universal itch to copulate, whose soul lusts only for disjunction? Even our modest

coupling (chaste beside *his* performances), rousing as it was
to tickly sense, went so counter to my principles I'd hardly
have enjoyed it even had my brother not indignified her the
while. Not content to be double already, he must attach
himself to everyone, everything; hug, devour, absorb! Heads
or tails, it's all one to Brother; he clamped his shaggy thighs
about the poor girl's ears as greedily as he engorges a potroast
or smothers me into the mattress, threatening with a laugh to
squash and ingest me.

After a series of such meetings (the film director, whether as
artist or as Teuton, was a perfectionist) we discovered ourselves in love: I with Thalia, my brother likewise in his
fashion, and laughing Thalia . . . with me, with me, I'm sure
of it! At least in the beginning. She joined our act, inspired or
composed fresh material for us; we played with profit the
naughty stages of a dozen nations, my brother still pretending
he had no brother despite our billing: *The Eternal Triangle.*
Arranged in parallel, isosceles, or alphaic fashion, we slept in
the same hotel beds, and while it was he who salivated and
grunted upon her night after night, as he does yet, still it
pleased me to imagine that Thalia permitted him her supple
favors out of love for me, and humored his pretense that I did
not exist in order to be with me. By gay example she taught
me to make fun of our predicament, chuckle through the
teeth of anguish, turn woe into wit. In the heights of his
barbarous passion our eyes meet, and I have seen her wink; as
he roars in his transports, her chin rests on his shoulder; she
grins, and I chastely kiss her brow. More than once I have
been moved to put my love into written words, to no avail;
what profit to be articulate, when he seizes every message like
a jealous censor and either obscures its tender sentiments past
deciphering or translates them into his own coarse idiom? I
reach to comfort her; he thrusts my hand into her crotch; she
takes it for his and pretends delight. Agile creature that she is,
she would enfold us both in her honey limbs, so to touch the

one she loves; as if aware, he thwarts her into some yoga position, Bandha Padmāsana, Dhanurāsana. Little wonder our love remains tentative with him between us, who for aught I know may garble even this petition; little wonder we doubt and mistake each other. Indeed, I can only forgive her, however broken-heartedly, if the worst of my suspicions should prove true: that, hardened by despair, Thalia is becoming her disguise: the vulgar creature who ignores my signals, denies my presence, growls with feral joy beneath her ravisher! My laughter sticks in my throat; either Thalia has lost her sense of humor or I've lost mine. Mirth passes; our wretchedness endures and brutalizes. Truth to tell, she has become a stranger; with the best will in the world I can't always persuade my heart that her refusal to acknowledge me is but a stratagem of love, her teasing and fondling of the man I abhor mere feminine duplicity, to inspire my ardor and cover our tracks. What tracks, Thalia? Of late, particularly, she behaves on occasion as if *I* stood in the way of her contentment, and in darkest moments I can even wonder whether her demand that my brother "pull himself together" is owing to her secret desire for me or a secret wish to see me gone.

This ultimatum she pronounced on our thirty-fifth birthday, three weeks past. We were vacationing between a profitable Mardi-Gras engagement in New Orleans and a scheduled post-Lenten tour of Western speakeasies; indeed, despite Prohibition and Depression, perhaps because of them, we'd had an uncommonly prosperous season; the demand for our sort of spectacle had never been so great; people crowded into basement caves to drink illicit liquors and applaud our repertoire of unnatural combinations and obscene gymnastics. One routine in particular was lining our pockets, a lubricious soft-shoe burlesque of popular songs beginning with *Me and My Shadow* and culminating in *When We're Alone*; it was Thalia's invention, and doubtless inspired both my

brother's birthday proposal and her response. She had
bought a cake to celebrate the occasion (for both of us, I was
sure, though seventy candles would clearly have been too
many); my brother, who ordinarily blew out all the candles
and clawed into the frosting with both hands before I could
draw a breath, had been distracted all day, and managed only
thirty-four; eagerly I puffed out the last, over his shoulder, my
first such opportunity in three decades and a half, whereat he
threw off his mood with a laugh and revealed his wish: to
join himself to Thalia in marriage. In his blurting fashion he
enounced a whole mad program: he would put the first half
of his life altogether behind him, quit show business, use our
savings to learn an honest trade, perhaps husbandry, perhaps
welding, and raise a family!

"Two can live cheap as one," he grumbled at the end—
somewhat defensively, for Thalia showed neither surprise,
pleasure, nor dismay, but heard him out with a neutral
expression as if the idea were nothing new. I searched her face
for assurance that she was revolted; I waved my arms and
shook my head, turned out my pockets to find the NO-sign I
always carried with me, so often was it needed, and flung it in
her direction when she wouldn't look at it. Long time she
studied him, twirling a sprig of ivy between her fingers; cross
with suspense, he admitted he'd been no model companion,
but a moody, difficult, irresolute fellow plagued with tensions and contradictions. I mouthed antic sneers over his
shoulders. But with her assistance he would become a new
man, he declared, and promised ominously to "get rid," "one
way or another," of "the monkey on his back," which had
kept him to date from single-minded application to anything. It was his first employment of the epithet; I shuddered
at his resolve. She was his hope of redemption, he went on,
becoming fatuous and sentimental now in his anxiety; without her he was no better than a beast (as if he weren't beastly
with her!), no more than half a man; let her but consent,

therefore and however, to become as the saying was his better half, he'd count himself saved!

Why did she not laugh in his face, throw up to him his bestialities, declare once for all that she endured him solely on my account? She rose from table, leaning upon the cane she always danced with; I held out my arms to her and felt on each elbow the tears my brother forced to dramatize his misery. Oh, he is a cunning animal! I even attempted tears myself, but flabbergastment dried my eyes. At the door Thalia turned to gaze as if it were through him—the last time, I confess, that I was able to believe she might be looking at me. Then bending with a grunt to retrieve my crumpled message, which she tossed unread into the nearest ashtray, she replied that she was indeed weary of acrobatics: let him make good his aforementioned promise, one way or another; then she'd see.

No sooner had she spoken than the false tears ceased; my brother chased her squealing into the kitchen, nor troubled even to ask her leave, but swinish as ever fetched down her tights with the cane-crook and rogered her fair athwart the dish drain, all the while snorting through her whoop and giggle: "You'll see what you'll see!"

Highness, I live in terror of what she'll see! Nothing is beyond my brother. He has put himself on a diet, avowedly to trim his grossness for her sake; but I perceive myself weaker in consequence, and am half-convinced he means to starve me on the vine, as it were, and absorb me through the bond that joins us. He has purchased medical insurance, playing the family man, and remarks as if idly on its coverage of massive skin grafts; for all I know he may be planning to install me out of sight inside him by surgical means. I don't eat; I daren't sleep. Thalia, my hope and consolation—why has she forsaken me?

If indeed she has. For a curious fancy has taken me of late, not impossibly the figment of a mind deranged for want of love (and rest, and sustenance): that Thalia is less simple than she appears. I suspect, in fact, or begin to ... that there are two Thalias! Don't mistake me: not two as Chang and Eng were two, or as my brother and I are two; not one Thalia joined to another—but a Thalia *within* a Thalia, like the dolls-within-dolls Your Majesty's countrymen and neighbors fashion so cleverly: a Thalia incarcerate in the iron maiden my brother embraces!

I first observed her not long after that fell birthday. No moraler for all his protestations, my brother has devised for our next performance a new stunt based on an old lubricity, and to "get the hang of it" (so he claims) sleeps now arsy-turvy with his "fiancée," like shoes in a box or the ancient symbol for Yang and Yin. Sometimes she rests her head on his knees, and thus it happened, late one night, that when I looked down upon the Thalia who'd betrayed me, I found her looking back, sleepless as I, upside down in the first spring moonlight. Yet lo, it was not the same Thalia! Her face—I should say, her sister's face—was inverted, but I realized suddenly that her eyes were not; it was a different woman, a stranger, who regarded me with upright, silent stare through the other's face. I perspired with dismay—my first experience of sweat. Luckily my brother slept, a-pitch with dreams. There was no mistaking it, another woman looked out at me from behind that mask: a prisoner like myself, whose gaze remained level and detached however her heartless warden grinned and grimaced. I saw her the next night and the next, earnest, mute; by day she disappears in the other Thalia; I live only for the night, to rehearse before her steadfast eyes the pity and terror of our situation. She it is (once separate like myself, it may be, then absorbed by her smirking sister) I now adore—if with small hope and much apprehension. Does she see me winking and waving, or is my face as strange to her as her sister's to me? Why does she gaze at me so evenly, as if in unremitting appraisal? Can she too be uncertain of my reality, my love? Too much to bear!

In any case, there's little time. "Thalia" grows restive; now that she has the upper hand with my brother she makes no bones about her reluctance to go back on the road, her yen for a little farm, her dissatisfaction with his progress in "making a man of himself" and the like. Last night, I swear it, I felt him straining to suck me in through our conjunction, and clung to the sheets in terror. Momently I expect him to play some unsuspected trump; have at me for good and all. When he does, I will bite through the tie that binds us and so kill us both. It is a homicide God will forgive, and my beloved will at least be free of what she suffers, through her sister, at my brother's hands.

Yet given the daily advances of science and the inspiring circumstance of Your Majesty's visit, I dare this final hope: that at your bidding the world's most accomplished surgeons may successfully divide my brother from myself, in a manner such that one of us at least may survive, free of the other. After all, we were both joined once to our unknown mother, and safely detached to begin our misery. Or if a bond to *something* is necessary in our case, let it be something more congenial and sympathetic: graft my brother's Thalia in my place, and fasten me . . . to my own navel, to anything but him, if the Thalia I love can't be freed to join me! Perhaps she has another sister. . . . Death itself I would embrace like a lover, if I might share the grave with no other company. To be one: paradise! To be two: bliss! But to be both and neither is unspeakable. Your Highness may imagine with what eagerness His reply to this petition is awaited by

Yours truly,

You Are Not I
Paul Bowles

Paul Bowles

(United States, b. 1910)

"He opened the world of Hip. He let in the murder, the drugs, the incest, the death of the Square ... the call of the orgy, the end of civilization." Thus Norman Mailer described American writer Paul Bowles, whose work has stirred such talents as Tennessee Williams, William Burroughs, Jack Kerouac, Truman Capote, and Allen Ginsberg.

Like his countryman Edgar Allan Poe, whose brooding vision he shares, Bowles attended the University of Virginia, but dropped out to study musical composition with Aaron Copeland. He supported himself as a composer of theatre and film music, collaborating with Orson Welles, Elia Kazan and William Saroyan while publishing several short stories.

In 1931 Gertrude Stein suggested that Bowles travel to Tangier, then an international zone. It was here that he came of age as a writer of fiction. In his autobiography, *Without Stopping* (1972), Bowles described his first impression of Morocco: "Like any Romantic, I had always been vaguely certain that during my life I should come into a magic place which, in disclosing its secrets, would give me wisdom and ecstasy—perhaps even death." North Africa is the setting for many of Bowles's stories and novels (*The Sheltering Sky* (1949), *The Spider's House* (1955), *Points in Time* (1982)), and Tangier remains his home to the present day.

Bowles's fascination with otherness is evident in such stories as "A Distant Episode," "Pages from Cold Point," and "You Are Not I," which detail, with meticulous aloofness, the relentless disintegration of a psyche—stories in which, as he says, "everything gets worse."

You Are Not I

You are not I. No one but me could possibly be. I know that, and I know where I have been and what I have done ever since yesterday when I walked out the gate during the train wreck. Everyone was so excited that no one noticed me. I became completely unimportant as soon as it was a question of cut people and smashed cars down there on the tracks. We girls all went running down the bank when we heard the noise, and we landed against the cyclone fence like a lot of monkeys. Mrs Werth was chewing on her crucifix and crying her eyes out. I suppose it hurt her lips. Or maybe she thought one of her daughters was on the train down there. It was really a bad accident; anyone could see that. The spring rains had dissolved the earth that kept the ties firm, and so the rails had spread a little and the train had gone into the ditch. But how everyone could get so excited I still fail to understand.

I always hated the trains, hated to see them go by down there, hated to see them disappear way off up the valley toward the next town. It made me angry to think of all those people moving from one town to another, without any right to. Whoever said to them: "You may go and buy your ticket and make the trip this morning to Reading. You will go past twenty-three stations, over forty bridges, through three tunnels, and still keep going, if you want to ,even after you get to Reading"? No one. I know that. I know there is no chief who says things like that to people. But it makes it pleasanter for me when I imagine such a person does exist. Perhaps it would be only a tremendous voice speaking over a public-address system set up in all the main streets.

When I saw the train down there helpless on its side like an old worm knocked off a plant, I began to laugh. But I held on to the fence very hard when the people started to climb out the windows bleeding.

I was up in the courtyard, and there was the paper wrapper off a box of Cheese Tid Bits lying on the bench. Then I was at the main gate, and it was open. A black car was outside at the curb, and a man was sitting in front smoking. I thought of speaking to him and asking him if he knew who I was, but I decided not to. It was a sunny morning full of sweet air and birds, I followed the road around the hill, down to the tracks. Then I walked up the tracks feeling excited. The dining car looked strange lying on its side with the window glass all broken and some of the cloth shades drawn down. A robin kept whistling in a tree above. "Of course," I said to myself. "This is just in man's world. If something real should happen, they would stop singing." I walked up and down along the cinder bed beside the track, looking at the people lying in the bushes. Men were beginning to carry them up toward the front end of the train where the road crosses the tracks. There was a woman in a white uniform, and I tried to keep from passing close to her.

I decided to go down a wide path that led through the blackberry bushes, and in a small clearing I found an old stove with a lot of dirty bandages and handkerchiefs in the rubbish around the base of it. Underneath everything was a pile of stones. I found several round ones and some others. The earth here was very soft and moist. When I got back to the train there seemed to be a lot more people running around. I walked close to the ones who were lying side by side on the cinders, and looked at their faces. One was a girl and her mouth was open. I dropped one of the stones in and went on. A fat man also had his mouth open. I put in a sharp stone that looked like a piece of coal. It occurred to me that I might not have enough stones for them all, and the cinders were too small. There was one old woman walking up and down wiping her hands on her skirt very quickly, over and over again. She had on a long black silk dress with a design of blue mouths stamped all over it. Perhaps they were supposed to be leaves but they were formed like mouths. She looked crazy to me and I kept clear of her. Suddenly I noticed a hand with rings on the fingers sticking out from under a lot of bent pieces of metal. I tugged at the metal and saw a face. It was a woman and her mouth was closed. I tried to open it so I could get a stone in. A man grabbed me by the shoulder and pulled at me. He looked angry. "What are you doing?" he yelled. "Are you crazy?" I began to cry and said she was my sister. She did look a little like her, and I sobbed and kept saying· "She's dead. She's dead." The man stopped looking so angry and pushed me along toward the head of the train, holding my arm tightly with one hand. I tried to jerk away from him. At the same time I decided not to say anything more except "She's dead" once in a while. "That's all right," the man said. When we got to the front end of the train he made me sit down on the grass embankment alongside a lot of other people. Some of them were crying, so I stopped and watched them.

It seemed to me that life outside was like life inside. There was always somebody to stop people from doing what they wanted to do. I smiled when I thought that this was just the opposite of what I had felt when I was still inside. Perhaps what we want to do is wrong, but why should they always be the ones to decide? I began to consider this as I sat there pulling the little new blades of grass out of the ground. And I thought that for once *I* would decide what was right, and do it.

It was not very long before several ambulances drove up. They were for us, the row of people sitting on the bank, as well as for the ones lying around on stretchers and overcoats. I don't know why, since the people weren't in pain. Or perhaps they were. When a great many people are in pain together they aren't so likely to make a noise about it, probably because no one listens. Of course I was in no pain at all. I could have told anyone that if I had been asked. But no one asked me. What they did ask me was my address, and I gave my sister's address because it is only a half hour's drive. Besides, I stayed with her for quite a while before I went away, but that was years ago, I think. We all drove off together, some lying down inside the ambulances, and the rest of us sitting on an uncomfortable bench in one that had no bed. The woman next to me must have been a foreigner; she was moaning like a baby, and there was not a drop of blood on her that I could see, anywhere. I looked her all over very carefully on the way, but she seemed to resent it, and turned her face the other way, still crying. When we got to the hospital we were all taken in and examined. About me they just said: "Shock," and asked me again where I lived. I gave them the same address as before, and soon they took me out again and put me into the front seat of a sort of station wagon, between the driver and another man, an attendant, I suppose. They both spoke to me about the weather, but I knew enough not to let myself be trapped that easily. I know how the simplest subject can suddenly twist around and choke you when you think you're quite safe. "She's dead," I said once, when we were halfway between the two towns. "Maybe not, maybe not," said the driver, as if he were talking to a child. I kept my head down most of the time, but I managed to count the gas stations as we went along.

When we arrived at my sister's house the driver got out and rang the bell. I had forgotten that the street was so ugly. The houses were built one against the other, all alike, with only a narrow cement walk between. And each one was a few feet lower than the other, so that the long row of them looked like an enormous flight of stairs. The children were evidently allowed to run wild over all the front yards, and there was no grass anywhere in sight, only mud.

My sister came to the door. The driver and she spoke a few words, and then I saw her look very worried very suddenly. She came out to the car and leaned in. She had new glasses, thicker than the others. She did not seem to be looking at me. Instead she said to the driver: "Are you *sure* she's all right?"

"Absolutely," he answered. "I wouldn't be telling you if she wasn't. She's just been examined all over up at the hospital. It's just shock. A good rest will fix her up fine." The attendant got out, to help me out and up the steps, although I could have gone perfectly well by myself. I saw my sister looking at me out of the corner of her eye the same as she used to. When I was on the porch I heard her whisper to the attendant: "She don't look well yet to *me*." He patted her arm and said: "She'll be fine. Just don't let her get excited."

"That's what they always said," she complained, "but she just *does*."

The attendant got into the car. "She ain't hurt at *all*, lady." He slammed the door.

"Hurt!" exclaimed my sister, watching the car. It drove off and she stood following it with her eyes until it got to the top of the hill and turned. I was still looking down at the porch floor because I wasn't sure yet what was going to happen. I often feel that something is about to happen, and when I do, I stay perfectly still and let it go ahead. There's no use wondering about it or trying to stop it. At this time I had no particular feeling that a special event was about to come out, but I did feel that I would be more likely to do the right thing if I waited and let my sister act first. She stood where she was, in her apron, breaking off the tips of the pussywillow stems that stuck out of the bush beside her. She still refused to look at me. Finally she grunted: "Might as well go on inside. It's cold out here." I opened the door and walked in.

Right away I saw she had had the whole thing rebuilt, only backward. There was always a hall and a living room, except that the hall used to be on the left-hand side of the living room and now it was on the right. That made me wonder why I had failed to notice that the front door was now at the right end of the porch. She had even switched the stairs and fireplace around into each other's places. The furniture was the same, but each piece had been put into the position exactly opposite to the way it had been before. I decided to say nothing and let her do the explaining if she felt like it. It occurred to me that it must have cost her every cent she had in the bank, and still it looked exactly the same as it had when she began. I kept my mouth shut, but I could not help looking around with a good deal of curiosity to see if she had carried out the reversal in every detail.

I went into the living room. The three big chairs around the center table were still wrapped in old sheets, and the floor lamp by the pianola had the same torn cellophane cover on its shade. I began to laugh, everything looked so comical backward. I saw her grab the fringe of the portiere and look at me hard. I went on laughing.

The radio next door was playing an organ selection. Suddenly my sister said: "Sit down, Ethel. I've got something to do. I'll be right back." She went into the kitchen through the hall and I heard the back door open.

I knew already where she was going. She was afraid of me, and she wanted Mrs Jelinek to come over. Sure enough, in a minute they both came in, and my sister walked right into the living room this time. She looked angry now, but she had nothing to say. Mrs Jelinek is sloppy and fat. She shook hands with me and said: "Well, well, old-timer!" I decided not to talk to her either because I distrust her, so I turned around and lifted the lid of the pianola. I tried to push down some keys, but the catch was on and they were all stiff and wouldn't move. I closed the lid and went over to see out the window. A little girl was wheeling a doll carriage along the sidewalk down the hill; she kept looking back at the tracks the wheels made when they left a wet part of the pavement and went onto a dry patch. I was determined not to let Mrs Jelinek gain any advantage over me, so I kept quiet. I sat down in the rocker by the window and began to hum.

Before long they started to talk to each other in low voices, but of course I heard everything they said. Mrs Jelinek said: "I thought they was keeping her." My sister said: "I don't know. So did I. But the man kept telling me she was all right. Huh! She's just the same." "Why, sure," said Mrs Jelinek. They were quiet a minute.

"Well, I'm not going to put up with it!" said my sister, suddenly. "I'm going to tell Dr Dunn what I think of him."

"Call the Home," urged Mrs Jelinek.

"I certainly am," my sister answered. "You stay here. I'll see if Kate's in." She meant Mrs Schultz, who lives on the other side and has a telephone. I did not even look up when she went out. I had made a big decision, and that was to stay right in the house and under no condition let myself be taken back there. I knew it would be difficult, but I had a plan I knew would work if I used all my will power. I have great will power.

The first important thing to do was to go on keeping quiet, not to speak a word that might break the spell I was starting to work. I knew I would have to concentrate deeply, but that is easy for me. I knew it was going to be a battle between my sister and me, but I was confident that my force of character and superior education had fitted me for just such a battle, and that I could win it. All I had to do was to keep insisting inside myself, and things would happen the way I willed it. I said this to myself as I rocked. Mrs Jelinek stood in the hall doorway with her arms folded, mostly looking out the front door. By now life seemed much clearer and more purposeful than it had in a long, long time. This way I would have what I wanted. "No one can stop you," I thought.

It was a quarter of an hour before my sister came back. When she walked in she had both Mrs Schultz and Mrs Schultz's brother with her, and all three of them looked a little frightened. I knew exactly what had happened even before she told Mrs Jelinek. She had called the Home and complained to Dr Dunn that I had been released, and he had been very much excited and told her to hold on to me by all means because I had not been discharged at all but had somehow *got out*. I was a little shocked to hear it put that way, but now that I thought of it, I had to admit to myself that that was just what I had done.

I got up when Mrs Schultz's brother came in, and glared at him hard.

"Take it easy, now, Miss Ethel," he said, and his voice sounded nervous. I bowed low to him: at least he was polite.

"'Lo, Steve," said Mrs Jelinek.

I watched every move they made. I would have died rather than let the spell be broken. I felt I could hold it together only by a great effort. Mrs Schultz's brother was scratching the side of his nose, and his other hand twitched in his pants pocket. I knew he would give me no trouble. Mrs Schultz and Mrs Jelinek would not go any further than my sister told them to. And she herself was terrified of me, for although I had never done her any harm, she had always been convinced that some day I would. It may be that she knew now what I was about to do to her, but I doubt it, or she would have run away from the house.

"When they coming?" asked Mrs Jelinek.

"Soon's they can get here," said Mrs Schultz.

They all stood in the doorway.

"I see they rescued the flood victims, you remember last night on the radio?" said Mrs Schultz's brother. He lit a cigarette and leaned back against the banisters.

The house was very ugly, but I already was getting ideas for making it look better. I have excellent taste in decoration. I tried not to think of those things, and said over and over inside my head: "Make it work."

Mrs Jelinek finally sat down on the couch by the door, pulled her skirt around her legs and coughed. She still looked red in the face and serious. I could have laughed out loud when I thought of what they were really waiting to see if they had only known it.

I heard a car door slam outside. I looked out. Two of the men from the Home were coming up the walk. Somebody else was sitting at the wheel, waiting. My sister went quickly to the front door and opened it. One of the men said: "Where is she?" They both came in and stood a second looking at me and grinning.

"Well, hel-*lo*!" said one. The other turned and said to my sister: "No trouble?" She shook her head. "It's a wonder you couldn't be more careful," she said angrily. "They get out like that, how do *you* know what they're going to do?"

The man grunted and came over to me. "Wanna come with us? I know somebody who's waiting to see you."

I got up and walked slowly across the room, looking at the rug all the way, with one of the men on each side of me. When I got to the doorway beside my sister I pulled my hand out of the pocket of my coat and looked at it. I had one of my stones in my hand. It was very easy. Before either of them could stop me I reached out and stuffed the stone into her mouth. She screamed just before I touched her, and just afterward her lips were bleeding. But the whole thing took a very long time. Everybody was standing perfectly still. Next, the two men had hold of my arms very tight and I was looking around the room at the walls. I felt that my front teeth were broken. I could taste blood on my lips. I thought I was going to faint. I wanted to put my hand to my mouth, but they held my arms. "This is the turning point," I thought.

I shut my eyes very hard. When I opened them everything was different and I knew I had won. For a moment I could not see very clearly, but even during that moment I saw myself sitting on the divan with my hands in front of my mouth. As my vision cleared, I saw that the men were holding my sister's arms, and that she was putting up a terrific struggle. I buried my face in my hands and did not look up again. While they were getting her out the front door, they managed to knock over the umbrella stand and smash it. It hurt her ankle and she kicked pieces of porcelain back into the hall. I was delighted. They dragged her along the walk to the car, and one man sat on each side of her in the back. She was yelling and showing her teeth, but as they left the city limits she stopped, and began to cry. All the same, she was really counting the service stations along the road on the way back to the Home, and she found there was one more of them than she had thought. When they came to the grade crossing near the spot where the train accident had happened, she looked out, but the car was over the track before she realized she was looking out the wrong side.

Driving in through the gate, she really broke down. They kept promising her ice cream for dinner, but she knew better than to believe them. As she walked through the main door between the two men she stopped on the threshold, took out one of the stones from her coat pocket and put it into her mouth. She tried to swallow it, but it choked her, and they rushed her down the hall into a little waiting room and made her give it up. The strange thing, now that I think about it, was that no one realized she was not I.

They put her to bed, and by morning she no longer felt like crying: she was too tired.

It's the middle of the afternoon and raining torrents. She is sitting on her bed (the very one I used to have) in the Home, writing all this down on paper. She never would have thought of doing that up until yesterday, but now she thinks she has become me, and so she does everything I used to do.

The house is very quiet. I am still in the living room, sitting on the divan. I could walk upstairs and look into her bedroom if I wanted to. But it is such a long time since I have been up there, and I no longer know how the rooms are arranged. So I prefer to stay down here. If I look up I can see the square window of colored glass over the stairs. Purple and orange, an hourglass design, only the light never comes in very much because the house next door is so close. Besides, the rain is coming down hard here, too.

The Case for the Defence
Graham Greene

Graham Greene

(England, b. 1904)

The theme of the double and the dualities of life recur often in Graham Greene's writing. His time in the British Secret Service gave him the experience to write some of the finest spy fiction in the genre, where, of course, doubles are the norm. His novel *The Human Factor*, along with John Le Carré's *A Perfect Spy* and Julian Mitchell's play *Another Country*, ranks among the finest portraits of the spy's double life.

In his autobiography, *Ways of Escape* (1980), Greene writes of actually having a *doppelgänger*, of having received "letters from strangers who remember me at a wedding I never attended, or serving a Mass I never served...." This double has even been photographed and appeared in newspapers in Geneva and Jamaica. Greene says there are reasons to believe this "other" to be a certain jail breaker, John Skinner, or a man wanted by the police, Meredith de Varg. He concludes, "I found myself shaken by metaphysical doubt. Had I been the imposter all the time? Was I the Other? Was I Skinner? Was it even possible that I might be Meredith de Varg?"

If Greene has never actually written a pure detective story, he has maintained an interest in the form both as a bibliographer of detective stories and as a playwright (*The Return of A. J. Raffles*). In "A Case for the Defence," he poses the question raised in all murder mysteries: "Who done it?" Well, jury...

The Case for the Defence

It was the strangest murder trial I ever attended. They named it the Peckham murder in the headlines, though Northwood Street, where the old woman was found battered to death, was not strictly speaking in Peckham. This was not one of those cases of circumstantial evidence in which you feel the jurymen's anxiety—because mistakes *have* been made—like domes of silence muting the court. No, this murderer was all but found with the body; no one present when the Crown counsel outlined his case believed that the man in the dock stood any chance at all.

He was a heavy stout man with bulging bloodshot eyes. All his muscles seemed to be in his thighs. Yes, an ugly customer, one you wouldn't forget in a hurry—and that was an important point because the Crown proposed to call four witnesses who hadn't forgotten him, who had seen him hurrying away from the little red villa in Northwood Street. The clock had just struck two in the morning.

Mrs Salmon in 15 Northwood Street had been unable to sleep, she heard a door click shut and thought it was her own gate. So she went to the window and saw Adams (that was his name) on the steps of Mrs Parker's house. He had just come out and he was wearing gloves. He had a hammer in his hand and she saw him drop it into the laurel bushes by the front gate. But before he moved away, he had looked up—at her window. The fatal instinct that tells a man when he is watched exposed him in the light of a street-lamp to her gaze —his eyes suffused with horrifying and brutal fear, like an animal's when you raise a whip. I talked afterwards to Mrs Salmon, who naturally after the astonishing verdict went in fear herself. As I imagine did all the witnesses—Henry Mac-Dougall, who had been driving home from Benfleet late and nearly ran Adams down at the corner of Northwood Street. Adams was walking in the middle of the road looking dazed. And old Mr Wheeler, who lived next door to Mrs Parker, at No. 12, and was awakened by a noise—like a chair falling— through the thin-as-paper villa wall, and got up and looked out of the window, just as Mrs Salmon had done, saw Adams's back and, as he turned, those bulging eyes. In Laurel Avenue he had been seen by yet another witness—his luck was badly out; he might as well have committed the crime in broad daylight.

"I understand," counsel said, "that the defence proposes to plead mistaken identity. Adams's wife will tell you that he was with her at two in the morning on February 14, but after you have heard the witnesses for the Crown and examined carefully the features of the prisoner, I do not think you will be prepared to admit the possibility of a mistake."

It was all over, you would have said, but the hanging.

After the formal evidence had been given by the policeman who had found the body and the surgeon who examined it, Mrs Salmon was called. She was the ideal witness, with her slight Scotch accent and her expression of honesty, care and kindness.

The counsel for the Crown brought the story gently out.

She spoke very firmly. There was no malice in here, and no sense of importance at standing there in the Central Criminal Court with a judge in scarlet hanging on her words and the reporters writing them down. Yes, she said, and then she had gone downstairs and rung up the police station.

"And do you see the man here in court?"

She looked straight at the big man in the dock, who stared hard at her with his Pekingese eyes without emotion.

"Yes," she said, "there he is."

"You are quite certain?"

She said simply, "I couldn't be mistaken sir."

It was all as easy as that.

"Thank you, Mrs Salmon."

Counsel for the defense rose to cross-examine. If you had reported as many murder trials as I have, you would have known beforehand what line he would take. And I was right, up to a point.

"Now, Mrs Salmon, you must remember that a man's life may depend on your evidence."

"I do remember it, sir."

"Is your eyesight good?"

"I have never had to wear spectacles, sir."

"You are a woman of fifty-five?"

"Fifty-six, sir."

"And the man you saw was on the other side of the road?

"Yes, sir."

"And it was two o'clock in the morning. You must have remarkable eyes, Mrs Salmon?"

"No, sir. There was moonlight, and when the man looked up, he had the lamplight on his face."

"And you have no doubt whatever that the man you saw is the prisoner?"

I couldn't make out what he was at. He couldn't have expected any other answer than the one he got.

"None whatever, sir. It isn't a face one forgets."

Counsel took a look round the court for a moment. Then he said, "Do you mind, Mrs Salmon, examining again the people in court? No, not the prisoner. Stand up, please Mr Adams," and there at the back of the court with thick stout body and muscular legs and a pair of bulging eyes, was the exact image of the man in the dock. He was even dressed the same—tight blue suit and striped tie.

"Now think very carefully, Mrs Salmon. Can you still swear that the man you saw drop the hammer in Mrs Parker's garden was the prisoner—and not this man, who is his twin brother?"

Of course she couldn't. She looked from one to the other and didn't say a word.

There the big brute sat in the dock with his legs crossed, and there he stood too at the back of the court and they both stared at Mrs Salmon. She shook her head.

What we saw then was the end of the case. There wasn't a witness prepared to swear that it was the prisoner he'd seen. And the brother? He had his alibi, too; he was with his wife.

And so the man was acquitted for lack of evidence. But whether—if he did the murder and not his brother—he was punished or not, I don't know. That extraordinary day had an extraordinary end. I followed Mrs Salmon out of court and we got wedged in the crowd who were waiting, of course, for the twins. The police tried to drive the crowd away, but all they could do was keep the road-way clear for traffic. I learned later that they tried to get the twins to leave by a back way, but they wouldn't. One of them—no one knew which—said, 'I've been acquitted, haven't I?' and they walked bang out of the front entrance. Then it happened. I don't know how, though I was only six feet away. The crowd moved and somehow one of the twins got pushed on to the road right in front of a bus.

He gave a squeal just like a rabbit and that was all; he was dead, his skull smashed just as Mrs Parker's had been. Divine vengeance? I wish I knew. There was the other Adams getting on his feet from beside the body and looking straight over at Mrs Salmon. He was crying, but whether he was the murderer or the innocent man nobody will ever be able to tell. But if you were Mrs Salmon, could you sleep at night?

The Dummy
Susan Sontag

Susan Sontag

(United States, b. 1933)

Susan Sontag is best known as a cultural critic and an incisive essayist who writes provocatively on the aesthetic experience. Her wide-ranging essays deal with film directors like Bergman, Godard, Resnais, and Syberberg, philosophers E.M. Cioran and Roland Barthes, and such subjects as fascism, pornography as an art form, and the nature of camp. She has published book-length essays in *Trip to Hanoi* (1968), *On Photography* (1977), and *Illness as Metaphor* (1978). But this stimulating body of commentary is only half the picture; she has also a dual career as film director and novelist. She wrote and directed two screenplays, *Duet for Cannibals* (1968) and *Brother Carl* (1970), and in 1973 directed a documentary film, *Promised Lands*, about the Yom Kippur War.

As a novelist and short story writer she has often dealt with the theme of duality. Her first novel, *The Benefactor* (1963), treats the relationship between the day-self and the night-self, reality and dream: Hippolyte, the young protagonist, becomes aware of the liberating effect of dreams and attempts to re-create in his daytime life the situations dreamed at night. *Death Kit* (1967) addresses a similar theme; having elements of a murder mystery, it may be read as a dream, a fantasy, or a straight narrative. The story "Doctor Jekyll" takes up Stevenson's famous yarn of exchanged identities. In "The Dummy," Sontag explores a kind of double first known as a golem, and whose most recent counterpart we call a robot. In Fritz Lang's film *Metropolis*, the inventor Rotwang boasts, "I have created a machine in the image of man, that never tires or makes a mistake." The protagonist in "The Dummy" chooses a like course, explaining, "The problems of the world are only truly solved in two ways: by extinction or by duplication."

The Dummy

Since my situation is intolerable, I have decided to take steps to resolve it. So I have constructed a lifelike dummy made of various brands of Japanese plastic simulating flesh, hair, nails, and so forth. An electronics engineer of my acquaintance, for a sizable fee, built the interior mechanism of the dummy: it will be able to talk, eat, work, walk, and copulate. I hired an important artist of the old realistic school to paint the features; it took twelve sittings to make a face that perfectly resembles mine. My broad nose is there, my brown hair, the lines on each side of my mouth. Even I could not tell the dummy and myself apart, were it not that from my peculiar vantage point it is quite obvious that he is he and that I am I.

What remains is to install the dummy in the center of my life. He will go to work instead of me, and receive the approval and censure of my boss. He will bow and scrape and be diligent. All I require of him is that he bring me the check every other Wednesday; I will give him carfare and money for his lunches, but no more. I'll make out the checks for the rent and the utilities, and pocket the rest myself. The dummy will also be the one who is married to my wife. He will make love to her on Tuesday and Saturday night, watch television with her every evening, eat her wholesome dinners, quarrel with her about how to bring up the children. (My wife, who also works, pays the grocery bills out of her salary.) I will also assign the dummy Monday night bowling with the team from the office, the visit to my mother on Friday night, reading the newspaper each morning, and perhaps buying my clothes (two sets—one for him, one for me). Other tasks I will assign as they come up, as I wish to divest myself of them. I want to keep for myself only what gives me pleasure.

An ambitious enterprise, you say? But why not? The problems of this world are only truly solved in two ways: by extinction or by duplication. Former ages had only the first choice. But I see no reason not to take advantage of the marvels of modern technology for personal liberation. I have a choice. And, not being the suicidal type, I have decided to duplicate myself.

On a fine Monday morning I wind the dummy up and set him loose, after making sure he knows what to do—that is, he knows just how I would behave in any familiar situation. The alarm goes off. He rolls over and pokes my wife, who wearily gets out of the double bed and turns off the alarm. She puts on her slippers and robe, then limps, stiff-ankled, into the bathroom. When she comes out and heads for the kitchen, he gets up and takes her place in the bathroom. He urinates, gargles, shaves, comes back into the bedroom and takes his clothes out of the dresser and closet, returns to the bathroom, dresses, then joins my wife in the kitchen. My children are already at the table. The younger girl didn't finish her homework last night, and my wife is writing a note of excuse to the teacher. The older girl sits haughtily munching the cold toast. "Morning, Daddy," they say to the dummy. The dummy pecks them on the cheek in return. Breakfast passes without incident, I observe with relief. The children leave. They haven't noticed a thing. I begin to feel sure my plan is going to work and realize, by my excitement, that I had greatly feared it would not—that there would be some mechanical failure, that the dummy would not recognize his cues. But no, everything is going right, even the way he folds *The New York Times* is correct; he reproduces exactly the amount of time I spent on the foreign news, and it takes him just as long to read the sports pages as it took me.

The dummy kisses my wife, he steps out the door, he enters the elevator. (Do machines recognize each other, I wonder.) Into the lobby, out the door, on the street walking at a moderate pace—the dummy has left on time, he doesn't have to worry—into the subway he goes. Steady, calm, clean (I cleaned him myself Sunday night), untroubled, he goes about his appointed tasks. He will be happy as long as I am satisfied with him. And so I will be, whatever he does, as long as others are satisfied with him.

Nobody notices anything different in the office, either. The secretary says hello, he smiles back as I always do; then he walks to my cubicle, hangs up his coat, and sits at my desk. The secretary brings him my mail. After reading it, he calls for some dictation. Next, there is a pile of my unfinished business from last Friday to attend to. Phone calls are made, an appointment is set up for lunch with a client from out of town. There is only one irregularity that I notice: the dummy smokes seven cigarettes during the morning; I usually smoke between ten and fifteen. But I set this down to the fact that he is new at his work and has not had time to accumulate the tensions that I feel after working six years in this office. It occurs to me that he will probably not have two martinis—as I always do—during the lunch, but only one, and I am right. But these are mere details, and will be to the dummy's credit if anyone notices them, which I doubt. His behavior with the out-of-town client is correct—perhaps a shade too deferential, but this too, I put down to inexperience. Thank God, no simple matter trips him up. His table manners are as they should be. He doesn't pick at his food, but eats with appetite. And he knows he should sign the check rather than pay with a credit card; the firm has an account at this restaurant.

In the afternoon there is a sales conference. The vice president explains a new promotional campaign for the Midwest. The dummy makes suggestions. The boss nods. The dummy taps his pencil on the long mahogany table and looks thoughtful. I notice he is chain-smoking. Could he be feeling the pressure so soon? What a hard life I led! After less than a day of it, even a dummy shows some wear and tear. The rest of the afternoon passes without incident. The dummy makes his way home to my wife and children, eats my dinner appreciatively, plays Monopoly with the children for an hour, watches a Western on TV with my wife, bathes, makes himself a ham sandwich, and then retires. I don't know what dreams he has, but I hope they are restful and pleasant. If my approval can give him an untroubled sleep, he has it. I am entirely pleased with my creation.

The dummy has been on the job for several months. What can I report? A greater degree of proficiency? But that's impossible. He was fine the first day. He couldn't be anymore like me than he was at the very beginning. He does not have to get better at his job but only stick at it contentedly, unrebelliously, without mechanical failure. My wife is happy with him—at least, no more unhappy than she was with me. My children call him Daddy and ask for their allowance. My fellow workers and my boss continue to entrust him with my job.

Lately, though—just the past week, really—I have noticed something that worries me. It is the attention that the dummy pays to the new secretary, Miss Love. (I hope it isn't her name that arouses him somewhere in the depths of that complex machinery; I imagine that machines can be literal-minded.) A slight lingering at her desk when he comes in in the morning, a second's pause, no more, when she says hello; whereas I— and he until recently—used to walk by that desk without breaking stride. And he does seem to be dictating more letters. Could it be from increased zeal on behalf of the firm? I remember how, the very first day, he spoke up at the sales conference. Or could it be the desire to detain Miss Love? Are those letters necessary? I could swear he thinks so. But then you never know what goes on behind that imperturbable dummy's face of his. I'm afraid to ask him. Is it because I don't want to know the worst? Or because I'm afraid he'll be angry at my violation of his privacy? In any case, I have decided to wait until he tells me.

Then one day it comes—the news I had dreaded. At eight in the morning the dummy corners me in the shower, where I have been spying on him while he shaves, marveling how he remembers to cut himself every once in a while, as I do. He unburdens himself to me. I am astonished at how much he is moved—astonished and a little envious. I never dreamed a dummy could have so much feeling, that I would see a dummy weep. I try to quiet him. I admonish him, then I reprimand him. It's no use. His tears become sobs. He, or rather his passion, whose mechanism I cannot fathom, begins to revolt me. I am also terrified my wife and children will hear him, rush to the bathroom, and there find this berserk creature who would be incapable of normal responses. (Might they find both of us here in the bathroom? That, too, is possible.) I run the shower, open both the sink faucets, and flush the toilet to drown out the painful noises he is making. All this for love! All this for the love of Miss Love! He has barely spoken to her, except in the way of business. Certainly, he hasn't slept with her, of that I am sure. And yet he is madly, desperately in love. He wants to leave my wife. I explain to him how impossible that is. First of all, he

has duties and responsibilities. He is the husband and father
to my wife and children. They depend on him; their lives
would be smashed by his selfish act. And second, what does
he know about Miss Love? She's at least ten years younger
than he is, has given no particular sign of noticing him at all,
and probably has a nice boyfriend her own age whom she's
planning to marry.

The dummy refuses to listen. He is inconsolable. He will
have Miss Love or—here he makes a threatening gesture—he
will destroy himself. He will bang his head against the wall,
or jump out of a window, disassembling irrevocably his
delicate machinery. I become really alarmed. I see my marvel-
lous scheme, which has left me so beautifully at my leisure
and in peace the last months, ruined. I see myself back at the
job, making love again to my wife, fighting for space in the
subway during the rush hour, watching television, spanking
the children. If my life was intolerable to me before, you can
imagine how unthinkable it has become. Why, if only you
knew how I have spent these last months, while the dummy
was administering my life. Without a care in the world,
except for occasional curiosity as to the fate of my dummy. I
have slid to the bottom of the world. I sleep anywhere now: in
flophouses, on the subway (which I only board very late at
night), in alleys and doorways. I don't bother to collect my
paycheck from the dummy any more, because there is nothing I want to buy. Only rarely do I shave. My clothes are torn
and stained.

Does this sound very dreary to you? It is not, it is not. Of
course, when the dummy first relieved me of my own life, I
had grandiose plans for living the lives of others. I wanted to
be an Arctic explorer, a concert pianist, a great courtesan, a
world statesman. I tried being Alexander the Great, then
Mozart, then Bismarck, then Greta Garbo, then Elvis Presley
—in my imagination, of course. I imagined that, being none
of these people for long, I could have only their pleasure,

none of their pain; for I could escape, transform myself, whenever I wanted. But the experiment failed, for lack of interest, from exhaustion, call it what you will. I discovered that I am tired of being a person. Not just tired of being the person I was, but any person at all. I like watching people, but I don't like talking to them, dealing with them, pleasing them, or offending them. I don't even like talking to the dummy. I am tired. I would like to be a mountain, a tree, a stone. If I am to continue as a person, the life of the solitary derelict is the only one tolerable. So you will see that it is quite out of the question that I should allow the dummy to destroy himself, and have to take his place and live my old life again.

I continue my efforts of persuasion. I got him to dry his tears and go out and face the family breakfast, promising him that we will continue our conversation in the office, after he dictates his morning batch of letters to Miss Love. He agrees to try, and makes his red-eyed, somewhat belated appearance at the table. "A cold, dear?" says my wife. The dummy blushes and mumbles something. I pray that he will hurry up. I am afraid he will break down again. I notice with alarm that he can hardly eat, and leaves his coffee cup two-thirds full.

The dummy makes his way sadly out of the apartment, leaving my wife perplexed and apprehensive. I see him hail a cab instead of heading for the subway. In the office, I eavesdrop as he dictates his letters, sighing between every sentence. Miss Love notices, too. "Why, what's the matter?" she asks cheerfully. There is a long pause. I peep out of the closet, and what do I see! The dummy and Miss Love in a hot embrace. He is stroking her breasts, her eyes are closed, with their mouths they wound each other. The dummy catches sight of me staring from behind the closet door. I signal wildly, trying to make him understand that we must talk, that I'm on his side, that I'll help him. "Tonight?" whispers the dummy, slowly releasing the ecstatic Miss Love. "I adore you," she whispers. "I adore you," says the dummy in a voice above a whisper, "and I must see you." "Tonight," she whispers back. "My place. Here's the address."

One more kiss and Miss Love goes out. I emerge from the closet and lock the door of the little office. "Well," says the dummy. "It's Love or death." "All right," I say sadly. "I won't try to talk you out of it any more. She seems like a nice girl. And quite attractive. Who knows, if she had been working here when I was here . . ." I see the dummy frowning angrily, and don't finish the sentence. "But you'll have to give me a little time," I say. "What are you going to do? As far as I can see, there's nothing you can do," says the dummy. "If you think I'm going home to your wife and kids anymore, after I've found Love—" I plead with him for time.

What do I have in mind? Simply this. The dummy is now in my original position. His present arrangements for life are intolerable to him. But having more appetite for a real, individual life than I ever had, he doesn't want to vanish from the world. He just wants to replace my admittedly second-hand wife and two noisy daughters with the delightful, childless Miss Love. Well then, why shouldn't my solution—duplication—work for him as it did for me? Anything is better than suicide. The time I need is time to make another dummy, one to stay with my wife and children and go to my job while this dummy (the true dummy, I must now call him) elopes with Miss Love.

Later that morning, I borrow some money from him to go to a Turkish bath and get cleaned up, to get a haircut and shave at the barber's, and to buy myself a suit like the one he is wearing. On his suggestion, we meet for lunch at a small restaurant in Greenwich Village, where it is impossible that he meet anyone who might recognize him. I'm not sure what he is afraid of. Of having lunch alone, and being seen talking to himself? Of being seen with me? But I am perfectly presentable now. And if we are seen as two, what could be more normal than a pair of identical adult male twins, dressed alike, having lunch together and engaged in earnest conversation? We both order spaghetti *al burro* and baked clams. After three drinks, he comes around to my point of view. In consideration of my wife's feelings, he says—not mine, he insists several times in rather harsh tone of voice—he will wait. But only a few months, no more. I point out that in this interim I will not ask that he not sleep with Miss Love but only that he be discreet in his adultery.

Making the second dummy is harder than making the first. My entire savings are wiped out. The prices of humanoid plastic and the other material, the fees of the engineer and the artist, have all gone up within just a year's time. The dummy's salary, I might add, hasn't gone up at all, despite the boss's increased appreciation of his value to the firm. The dummy is annoyed that I insist that he, rather than I, sit for the artist when the facial features are being molded and painted. But I point out to him that if the second dummy is modeled on me again, there is a chance that it would be a blurred or faded copy. Undoubtedly, some disparities have developed between the appearance of the first dummy and my own, even though I cannot detect them. I want the second dummy to be like him, wherever there is the slightest difference between him and me. I shall have to take the risk that in the second dummy might also be reproduced the unforeseen human passion that robbed the first dummy of his value to me.

Finally, the second dummy is ready. The first dummy, at my insistence (and reluctantly, since he wanted to spend his spare time with Miss Love), takes charge of his training and indoctrination period, lasting several weeks. Then the great day arrives. The second dummy is installed in the first dummy's life in the midst of a Saturday afternoon baseball game, during the seventh-inning stretch. It has been arranged

that the first dummy will go out to buy hot dogs and Cokes
for my wife and children. It is the first dummy who goes out,
the second who returns laden with the food and drinks. The
first dummy then leaps into a cab, off into the waiting arms
of Miss Love.

That was nine years ago. The second dummy is living with
my wife in no more exalted or depressed a fashion than I had
managed. The older girl is in college, the second in high
school; and there is a new child, a boy, now six years old.
They have moved to a co-op apartment in Forest Hills; my
wife has quit her job; and the second dummy is assistant vice
president of the firm. The first dummy went back to college
nights while working as a waiter during the day; Miss Love
also went back to college and got her teacher's license. He is
now an architect with a growing practice; she teaches English
at Julia Richman High School. They have two children, a
boy and a girl, and are remarkably happy. From time to time,
I visit both my dummies—never without sprucing myself up
first, you understand. I consider myself a relative and the
godfather, sometimes the uncle, of all their children. They are
not happy to see me, perhaps because of my shabby appearance, but they haven't the courage to turn me out. I never stay
long, but I wish them well, and congratulate myself for
having solved in so equitable and responsible a manner the
problems of this one poor short life that was allotted me.

The Expensive Delicate Ship
Brian W. Aldiss

Brian W. Aldiss

(England, b. 1925)

The innovative work of English science fiction writer Brian W. Aldiss owes more to surrealism, the French "antinovelists," James Joyce and G. I. Gurdjieff than to Flash Gordon, BEMS and outer space. In his literary tour de force *Report on Probability A* (1968), a group of "watchers" observe the nature of a world virtually identical with their own. Aldiss implies that time is static and that "reality" is in the eye of the beholder. He presents this reality as a multiple mirror reflecting worlds within worlds *ad infinitum*. The book concludes enigmatically; Aldiss provides no answers.

Aldiss has written two novels that mirror well-known literary predecessors. He pays homage to H. G. Wells in *Moreau's Other Island* (1980), and in *Frankenstein Unbound* (1973) his protagonist is thrown back in time to Switzerland just as Dr Frankenstein (or rather, Mary Shelley) animates the Creature. Aldiss's reader must become an active character and slay the monster—the double within us all.

The theme of doubling in effect becomes one of tripling in *Brothers of the Head* (1977), Aldiss's subtle tale about Siamese-twin rock stars with a third, dormant head that makes increasing demands for its right to selfhood.

Doubles are usually human, but in "The Expensive Delicate Ship," Aldiss not only suggests how we may have lost our fabulous beasts, but contrasts the rich diversity of life with the silence of death.

The Expensive Delicate Ship

But for him it was not an important failure; the sun shone
As it had on the white legs disappearing into the green
Water; and the expensive delicate ship that must have seen
Something amazing, a boy falling out of the sky,
Had somewhere to get to and sailed calmly on.

W. H. AUDEN

In the old days, there used to be a suspension bridge across from Denmark to Sweden, between Helsingør and Halsingborg. It's scrapped now. It became too dangerous. But it had a moving walkway, and my friend Göran Svenson and I often used to use it. At one time, taking the walkway grew into a pleasant afternoon habit.

We got on the bridge one day, complaining, as everyone does occasionally, about our jobs. "We work so damned hard," I said. "When do we have time to live?"

"I've got a theory," he said, "that it's the other way about."
When Göran announces that he has a theory, you can be

pretty sure that something crazy is going to come out. "I think we work so hard, and do all the other things we do, because living—just intense pure living—is far too painful to endure. Work is a panacea which dilutes life."

"Good old Göran, you mean life is worse than death, I suppose?"

"No, not worse certainly, but the next most severe thing to death. Life is like light. All living creatures seek the light, but a really hard intense white light can kill them. Pure life's like that."

"You're a fine one to talk about a pure life, you old lecher!"

He gave me a pained look and said, "For that, I shall tell you a story."

We climbed on to the accelerating rollers, and so up to the walkway proper. We were carried out over Helsingør docks, and at once the Øresund was beneath us, its grey waters looking placid from where we stood.

This is Göran's story, as near as I can recall to the way he told it, though I may have forgotten one or two of his weird jokes.

He was aware that he was on a boat in a fearful storm. He thought the boat was sailing up the Skagerrak toward Oslo Fjord but, if so, there must have been some sort of a power failure, because the interior of the ship was miserably lit by dim lanterns swinging here and there.

Maybe it was a cattle boat, to judge by the smell. He was making his way up the companionway when a small animal —possibly a wallaby—darted by. He nearly fell backwards, but the ship pitched him forward at just the right moment, and he regained his balance.

When he got on deck—my God! What a sea! It couldn't be the Skagerrak; the Skagerrak was never that rough! Göran had spent several years at sea before the last vessels were completely automated, but he had never encountered an ocean like this. The air was almost as thick with water as the sea, so furiously was rain dashing down, blown savagely by high winds. There was no sign of coast, no glimpse of other vessels.

An old man made his way up to Göran, going hand-over-fist along the rails. His robes were dripping water. Something about his wild ancient look gave Göran a painful start. What sort of vessel was he aboard? He realized that the rails were made of wood, and the companionway, and the entire ship as far as he could see—roughly made, at that!

The old man clutched his arm and bellowed, "Get up to the wheel as fast as you can! Shem needs a hand!"

Göran could smell strong liquor on the old man's breath.

"Where are we?" he asked.

The old man laughed drunkenly. "In the world's pisspot, I should reckon! What a night! The windows of Heaven are open and the waters of Earth prevail exceedingly!"

As if to emphasize his words, a great mountain of water as big as an alp went bursting by, soaking them both completely.

"How—how long's this storm likely to last?" Göran asked.

"Why, long as the good Lord pleases! What a night! I've got the chimps working the pumps. Even the crocodiles are seasick! Keep your weather-eye open for a rainbow, that's all I can say. Now get to the wheel, fast as you can! I'm going below to secure the rhinos."

Göran had to fight his way first uphill and then downhill as the clumsy tub of a boat wallowed its way through the biggest storm since the world was created. He knew now that the Skagerrak would be a mere puddle compared to this all-encompassing ocean. They sailed on a planet without harbour or land to obstruct wind and wave. Small wonder the seas were so monstrous!

Forward, Shem was almost exhausted. Between them, the two men managed to lash the wheel to hold it. Every moment was a fight against elemental forces. The cries of animals and the groan of timbers were almost lost in the roaring wind, picked up and scattered contemptuously into the tempest.

Finally, between them, they had the ship heading into the storm, and clung to the wheel gasping for breath.

Göran thought himself beyond further fear when the ship was lifted high up a great sliding mountainside of water, up, up, to perch over a fearful gulf between waves. Just before they sliced down into the gulf, he saw a light ahead.

"Ship ahoy!" That was Shem, poor lad, pointing a finger in the direction Göran had been looking.

Ship? What ship? What possible ship could be sailing these seas at this time? What para-legendary voyage might it be on?

The two men stared at each other with pallid faces, and in one voice bellowed aloud for Noah. Then they turned to peer through the murk again.

At this point in his narrative, my friend Svenson broke off, to all appearances overcome by emotion. By now, the bridge had carried us half way across to Sweden; beneath us sailed the maritime traffic of the tranquil Øresund. But Göran's inner eye was fixed on another rougher sea.

"Did you catch a second glimpse of the phantom ship?" I asked.

You've no idea what it was like to sail that sea! The water was not like sea water. It was black, a black shot through with streaks of white and yellow, as if it were a living organism with veins and sinews. There were areas where fetid bubbles kept bursting to the surface, covering the waves with a vile foam . . .

Yes, we saw that phantom vessel again. Indeed we did! As the ark struggled up the mile-long side of yet another mountain of water, the other vessel came rushing down the slope upon us.

It was as fleet, as beautiful, as our tub was heavy and crude, was that expensive delicate ship! And it was lit from stem to stern; whereas the ark—that old fool Noah had not thought to provide navigational lights, reckoning his would be the only boat braving those high waters.

We stared aghast, Shem and I, as that superb craft bore down on us, much as two children in an alpine valley might gaze at the avalanche plunging down to destroy them.

Japheth had fought his way through the gale to cling beside us. His arrival made no impression on my consciousness until I heard him scream and turned to see his face—so pale and wet it seemed luminescent—and it was only on seeing him that I could realize the extent of my own terror!

"Where's your father? Where is he?" I shouted, seizing him by the shoulders.

"He stubbed his foot down below!"

Stubbed his foot! In sudden wild anger, I flung Japheth from me and, turning, pulled out my sheath knife. With a few slashes, I had cut the wheel free and flung it over with all my might, fighting the great roar of tide under our keel with every fibre of my being.

Sluggishly, our old tub turned a few degrees—and that great beautiful ship went racing by us to port, slicing up foam high over our poop, missing us, as it seemed, by inches!

It went by, and, as it went by—towering over us, that incredible ship—I saw a human face peer out at me. For the briefest moment, our gaze met. I tell you, it was the gaze of

doom. Well, such was my deep and ineradicable impression
—the gaze of doom!

Then it was gone, and I saw other faces, faces of animals,
all staring helplessly across the churning waters. Those animals—it was an instant's glimpse, no more, yet I know what
I saw! Unicorns, gryphons, a centaur with lashing mane, and
those superb beasts we have learned to call by Latin names—
megatherium, stegosaurus, a tyrannosaur, triceratops with
beaked mouth agape, diplodocus . . .

Of course, they all sliced by in a flash as the miraculous
ship—that doppelganger ark!—sped down the waters. And
then they were lost in the murk and spume. A flicker of light,
and once more our ark was all alone in the hostile sea, with
the windows of Heaven open upon us.

And I was wrestling with the wheel, on and on—maybe for
ever . . .

I burst out laughing.

"Great story, great performance! You are trying to persuade me that you sailed on the ark with Noah? Who were
you? Ham, no doubt!"

He looked pained.

"You see, you are so coarse, old chap! Your scepticism does
you no credit. Concentrate your attention on that fine ship
which almost rammed us. What was it? Where was it sailing?
Who built it? And what happened to it, what happened to all
the creatures aboard?"

"An even bigger mystery—did poor old Noah's toe get
better?"

He made a gesture of disgust. "You refuse to take me
seriously. Just consider the tragedy, the poetry, the mystery, of
that apocalyptic encounter. I sometimes ask myself if the
wrong vessel survived that gigantic storm. Remember that
God was very angry with that drunken old sot, Noah. Did the

wrong set of men and animals survive to repopulate the Earth?"

"I can't imagine a pterodactyl bringing a sprig of olive back into the ark."

"Laugh if you will! Sometimes I wonder what alternate possibilities and possible worlds flashed past my eyes in that moment of crisis. You haven't my fine imaginative mind— such speculations would mean nothing to you."

"You began this sermon by talking about just pure intense living—I suppose in contrast with all the muddled stuff we get through. Are you saying that this moment when you saw this—'doppelganger ark', as you call it, was a moment of intense living?"

He glanced down at the docks of Halsingborg, now rolling under our feet. The new art museum loomed ahead. We had almost arrived on the Swedish shore.

"No, not at all. Being so imaginative, my moment of intense living was to invent this little mysterious anecdote for you. I live in imagination! Too bad you are too much of a slob to appreciate it!"

Then he dropped his solemn expression and began to laugh. Roaring with laughter, we moved down the escalator to terra firma.

Next day, we saw in the newscasts that two small children, a boy and a girl, had been drowned in the Øresund just outside Halsingborg harbour, and at about the time we were passing regardlessly overhead.

Doubles
Alberto Moravia

Alberto Moravia

(Italy, b. 1907)

Alberto Moravia holds a place of prominence in twentieth-century literature as the author of the first existential novel, *Gli indifferenti*, (The Time of Indifference), which, published in 1929, predated both Sartre's *Nausea* and Camus's *The Outsider*. The Moravia family name was originally Pincherle, and this remains the author's middle name today; the confusion has caused some critics and bibliographers to conclude, erroneously, that "Moravia" is a pseudonym.

Duality, especially sexual duality, is a theme central to Moravia's work (*Two Adolescents, The Empty Canvas, Two Women*), and nowhere does he explore this better than in his savage comedy, *The Two of Us* (1972). The protagonist, Federico, a middle-aged script writer, has been endowed with a sexual organ of enormous size and rapacity; it also has the capacity of speech. Federico and "he" hold lengthy converse on sex, life and death, and "he" continually thrusts Federico, who practises chastity in the belief that sexual exertion drains the creative talent, into wilder and wilder situations. This struggle between Federico and his unruly member explores the fears and the dilemma of masculinity versus creativity.

Another Federico, Federico Fellini, wrote in *Oggi Illustrato*, "A mind that seeks to remain cool, lucid and well ordered like Moravia's seems to me comforting and reassuring, ready as it is to give a meaning to things and to treat them in a way that is human and useful." In "Doubles," Signori Fabiani/Mariani find such comfort in their double life.

Doubles

One day recently I came to a decision. I picked out an advertisement in which a "good room, sunny, bathroom; friendly atmosphere" was offered at an address a very long way from my own; I got into my car and went there. I live in a turning off the Via Cassia, almost in the country; the room of the advertisement was in a turning off the Via Appia Nuova: so great a distance seemed to me a safe guarantee of independence, secrecy and, above all, dissimilarity.

I myself did not know precisely what I wanted to do. Was I to embark seriously on a double life, with two homes, one near the Via Cassia and one near the Via Appia? I was a student, with my family in the provinces, and it would be easy to make each landlady believe that I had to spend fifteen days out of thirty in the country. Or was I, on the other hand, merely to take a look at the double life, but without—for the moment, anyhow—practising it? To sound out its possibilities, to get the taste of it?

Yes, that was it; because I did not desire a double life with the object of giving vent to some unavowable instinct; I did

not aspire, let us say, to be a faithful fiancé on the Via Cassia
and a Don Juan on the Via Appia. No, I had nothing to hide
or to give vent to in secret; I merely wished to duplicate
myself, that is, to become two people instead of one—and
indeed by doing the most innocent and normal things. The
double life, in fact, was for me not a means but an end.

I found the house of the advertisement in a turning off the
Via Appia that very much resembled the street in which I
lived near the Via Cassia: two rows of modern buildings, the
surface of the road uneven and full of holes and hummocks
and, at the far end, a strip of blue sky above a strip of green
countryside. Moreover the building itself was like the one in
which I lived: the same eight-storey façade riddled with windows and balconies, the same marble entrance-hall, the same
lift-shaft, the same staircase, the same balustrade. I reflected
that this, after all, was not so very strange: the building had
probably been constructed with the same materials, at the
same period, perhaps even by the same firm and according to
the plans of the same engineer. I reached the fourth floor. I
could hardly believe my eyes when I saw that the nameplate
bore the name of my Via Cassia landlady: "Longo." Then I
reflected that this was not an entirely improbable coincidence: Longo was not an uncommon name; in the telephone
directory there was a page and a half of Longos. I rang the
bell.

As I waited I was conscious of the same secret feeling of
expectation that I had experienced when I rang at the door of
Signora Longo No. 1, near the Via Cassia. Moreover this
feeling of expectation had not been falsified, for the door had
been opened by the lady's daughter, Elena, with whom I had
lost no time in forming a mildly amorous relationship. And
now the door opened and a gentle voice said: "Yes, what is
it?"

I looked up. Elena was fair, this one was dark; Elena's face
bore all the signs of health, with its blue eyes, pink cheeks

and scarlet mouth; this girl, on the other hand, had a delicate, pale, almost wasted face with two enormous dark, shining eyes. But the welcome was the same: discreet, reticent, even shy, but not indifferent—the usual welcome of a girl who finds herself confronted by a young man of her own age.

I explained what I wanted. She at once showed me into the sitting-room, announced that she would go and tell her mother, and disappeared. I looked round: in the home of Signora Longo No. 1 the predominant style was sham Renaissance; here it was sham Louis XVI; but I felt that this dissimilarity was only apparent and that, like the two Longo daughters, these two styles of decoration had, as far as concerned me, the same "intention." What this "intention" might be, I could not have said; but that it was the same, I was certain. I sat down and then almost shuddered as I recalled that Elena, too, had said, that day: "I'll go and tell Mother."

Soon the mother appeared. The same phenomenon was again repeated with regard to her as had formerly occurred in the case of Signora Longo No. 1: I did not see her. I was indeed aware that I had in front of me something mellifluous, homely, provincial, calculating and authoritative; but I failed to see what kind of a face and figure Signora Longo No. 2 had, just as, even now, I did not know what Signora Longo No. 1 looked like. Of course we all know that there are people who may even have an intense, though concealed, life, but who nevertheless make no more effect than a damp stain on a wall.

Anyhow, the following dialogue took place between us. "You are a student?"

"Yes, I'm studying literature."

"And your family, where are they?"

"At Ancona."

"A fine city, Ancona. I have a cousin at Ancona. Are you an only son?"

"Yes."

"I'm afraid you must be terribly spoilt, then. You only children . . . For example, my Elena . . ."

I gave a start. "Who is Elena?"

"My daughter."

"Excuse me. You were saying?"

"Ah yes, I was saying that, alas, Elena too is an only child."

"Why alas?"

"I should have liked so much to have a son. I always let the room to young men like you. Then I can partly deceive myself into thinking I have a son."

"I knew that too"; the remark escaped me.

"What?"

"I knew that you wanted so much to have a son and, not having one, that you let the room to young men like me."

"Excuse me, but how did you come to know that?"

"Well, I guessed it, when you told me that Elena is an only daughter and when I saw you sigh."

"You're very intuitive, there's no denying it. Anyhow, don't worry: here you'll be like one of the family, but at the same time you'll be free, perfectly free. Would you like to see the room?"

"Thank you, yes."

We went out into the passage; there was a door open, and at the far end of a long, narrow room, facing the window, Elena No. 2 was sitting at her desk. Her mother, as we went past, said: "Elena, let me introduce Signor . . . What is your name? Excuse me."

"Fabiani."

"Signor Fabiani, who is very soon coming to stay with us here."

Elena jumped up and at once came towards us, as though she were merely waiting to be called. We shook hands, and I noticed that, during my conversation with her mother, Elena had changed her clothes. When she had opened the door to me, she had been wearing a little green dress, rather shabby; now she had put on a red blouse and a grey skirt, both of which looked new. She followed us, and we went into the room, all three of us.

"The room is both light and quiet; on fine days you can see the Castelli Romani; this is the bathroom; all the furniture is new; this way, by this door, you can go in and out without anyone noticing." Signora Longo No. 2 went backwards and forwards, opening the windows, displaying drawers and cupboards, exactly as Signora Longo No. 1 had formerly done. And, as then, Elena stood aside looking at us; and I, instead of looking at the furniture and the landscape, looked at Elena. Then the repeated ringing of the telephone-bell was heard, and her mother said she was going to answer it and went out, leaving us alone.

I was standing near the door; Elena was at the other end of the room, near the window. We looked at one another, exactly as, in analogous circumstances (but that time it had been the front door bell) in the Longo No. 1 home, I and the other Elena had looked at one another. And in that moment, as with the other Elena, I realized that the girl was begging me to take the room and that I was promising her that I would do so. I felt that I had fallen on my feet; or rather that, just as the materials used, the plan adopted, the engineer and the firm entrusted with the job had brought it about that the building in which I found myself at the moment was in every respect similar to the one in which I lived near the Via Cassia; so, in the same way, an incommensurable number of forces were bringing it about that I should behave with Elena No. 2 in precisely the same way as I had behaved with Elena No. 1. Then, suddenly, an idea occurred to me: *this* was the double life, not that entirely different life that I had pictured. A life, that is, whose principal quality was not so much to change by changing its place and its circumstances, as to remain substantially identical. The feeling of duplication at which I had aimed was, fundamentally, just this: to acquire the consciousness, in doing something, that I had done it already and that anyhow it was impossible for me not to do it in precisely that way and no other.

This reflection lasted no more than a second. Then Signora Longo came back into the room, saying: "Wrong number."

There was nothing left for me but to go away. I told Signora Longo that I would give her my answer next day, I shook hands with Elena who left her hand in mine perhaps a moment longer than was necessary (as the other Elena had done); then I went down to the ground floor in the lift that was so like the one in the building near Via Cassia, even to the rude words scrawled on the glossy wood with the point of a nail.

I returned home. Scarcely had I thrown myself down on my bed, tired after so many adventures, when there was a knock at my door and Elena's voice said: "Telephone."

As I went out to take the call, Elena followed me and, while I was telephoning, took my hand and played with my fingers. At the other end of the line I heard the voice of the other Elena say: "Signor Fabiani?"

"Yes?"

"My mother asks me to tell you that there's no need for you to give her an answer. There was someone under consideration before you, and my mother has decided to let this other person have the room."

I enquired at once, hurriedly: "Who is this someone?"

"A student called Mariani."

"Ah, a student. And what's he like? Dark, fair, tall, short—what's he like?"

"You're rather strange, aren't you? He's more or less like you, neither dark nor fair, neither tall nor short, so-so. But why d'you want to know?"

"Thank you, I'm sorry, good-bye." I hung up the receiver:
Elena came close to me and said in a whisper: "Who was that
woman? What is there between you and her?"

I should have liked to reply: "That woman was you.
Between me and her there is exactly what there is between you
and me. Or rather, the student Mariani, who is so like me,
does with her what I should have been able to do, and so
there's no need for me to take the room off the Via Appia
since he will see to doing everything for me. And all of us, if
we want to, can live not merely two lives at the same time but
millions; all that's necessary is for us to be aware that we're
identical with millions of other people in the world." But I
thought she would not understand me and so I answered her
with a lie of some kind and went back to my room and threw
myself down on the bed again. It occurred to me that at that
very moment an infinite number of other people like me were
throwing themselves on their beds and, strange to say, this
thought comforted me, and, still thinking that I was doing
something that so many others were doing, I fell asleep.

Translated from the Italian by Angus Davidson

Twins
Eric McCormack

Eric McCormack

(Canada, b. 1940)

"These are magical journeys. This is an enticingly diabolical imagination." Thus has poet Susan Musgrave described the bizarre stories of Canadian writer Eric McCormack. Born in a small village in Scotland, he was "fetched" to Canada twenty-six years later by a land known to him only through films, television, and books.

McCormack's stories often reflect a preoccupation with doubles. In "Edward and Georgina," a brother and sister apparently cohabit, until on Edward's death it is discovered that he created Georgina—and masqueraded as her—out of loneliness. In "The Fugue," one man sets out to kill another, who happens to be reading a murder mystery in which the same scene is occurring.

It has been said, "Being a twin is like having a walking mirror." In "Twins," McCormack explores the horror of having another self —but here the twins must share a single body.

Twins

People swarm from north and south, abandon the rituals of Saturday afternoon shopping expeditions and ball-game attendances, in favour of him. One thing: no children. He demands no admission fee, so he is entitled to say "No children." ("Say" won't do. Even that woman, his mother, the crutch on which he has limped his eighteen years, can never be sure of what he "says." He, therefore, writes. And has written, with his right hand, and with his left hand, "NO CHILDREN.") For children are always the enemy: they suspect something, frown at him, tire of his performances, spoil everything. (As for dogs, they are wary too when they see him out walking. They sheath their tails. They slink growling to the opposite side of the road.) But, ah! The adults! The benches of the old church hall sag under the weight of their veneration. His devotees. How they admire him, how they nod their approval of his enigmatic sermons. He bestows upon them tears perhaps of gratitude, howls perhaps of execration. Either way, his votaries (the tall man with the blue eyes sits among them) are content.

The name of the one they come to hear? Malachi. That, at least, is sure. He has a sickness (is there a name for it?). His sickness attracts them. He is the one who speaks with two voices, two different voices, at the same time. One of the voices trolls smoothly from the right side of his mouth. The other crackles from the left corner. How memorable, how remarkable, the sound of those two voices emanating from that one flexible mouth.

Is his affliction, then, a miracle? No matter, it certainly complicates his life. It might be easier to bear if the two voices would speak in turns. But whenever he wants to say something, both voices chime in, overlap, each using an exactly equal number of syllables. Without euphony. There is discord in the sounds, there is dissent in the things said. What allures is the eeriness of it. The right-side voice thanks the tall man with the blue eyes for a gift he has brought:

"Thanks a lot."

But the left-side voice remarks simultaneously:

"You're a fool."

(Or is it vice versa? Often it is hard to tell.) The hearing is a difficult experience. Words sometimes twine together, like this—

```
"t          k         o
   h     n     s    l    t
     a              a
       r  e       o   o
       o  u      a  f     l
y"
```

—braided like two snakes. Or a discrepancy in timing produces a long, alien word: *"thyaounksreaalfoolot."* Or exact synchronization causes a triple grunt: *"th$_y$a$_{ou}$nks$_{re}$a$_a$l$_{fo}$ot$_{ol}$."* Leaving the hearer to rummage among fragments of words, palimpsests of phrases. Did he hear, "you're a lot," "thanks a fool," "yanks a lol," "thou're a foot?"

A disease of words. When Malachi was a child, nobody was willing to diagnose his problem. No father to turn to. His mother never revealed who fathered him in the bed of her clapboard house, imitation brick, a mile north of town. Malachi squirmed out of the womb, purple. Let loose his inhuman shrieks. It was presumed his brain was not right.

See him at the age of ten. A boy unable to cope with anything scholastic. No one understands his noises, the drooling, the maddening grunts. Then, lying on the floor on a Sunday morning in June, in his mother's presence, tiger stripes of sun through the shutters on his prone body, he who has never written a word, picks up two pencils, one in each hand, and writes two messages simultaneously on a sheet of paper. With his right hand, a neat firm line:

"Help me, Mother."

With his left hand a scrawl:

"Leave me alone."

She stares at the paper, squints at his mouth, understands at last. The why of it? How can such a thing have happened to her son? She expounds her theory to the tall man. (He has blue eyes, fine lines web the corners.) Malachi, she says, is meant to be twins, but somehow the division has not occurred, and he has been born, two people condemned to one body. Reverse Siamese twins. When she speaks of her theory in Malachi's presence, his face seems to confirm it. The right side blooms smooth, an innocent boy's. The left side shimmers with defiance. His head becomes unsteady, wobbles like an erratic planet with orbiting satellite eyes.

The German pastor is the force behind the audiences. He has spoken at some length to the tall man with the unflinching blue eyes. The pastor suggests to the mother that it will be good for the boy's confidence to exhibit himself. Is the pastor concerned about therapy or theology? Is he convinced that ultimately one voice or the other will prevail in open combat? Is he enthusiastic because he himself marvels at the sight? (Understands something?) He never misses an audience, sits rapt, engrossed in the turmoil in the face, the voice, of Malachi.

A sudden change. In the middle of the eighteenth year, tranquillity. The harsh voice silent, the soft voice alone emerges from the twisted mouth, unencumbered. The left side of the mouth still curls, the left cheek still twitches, the left eye still glares. People still cringe ready for the snarl. But they wait in vain. And Malachi appears one morning wearing a black cloth patch over the left side of his face. A black triangle.

They ask him, "What has happened to your other voice?"

He seems surprised at the question, as though unaware of the years of struggle. Soon, no one asks him any more, everyone becomes used to his masked face. They admire it, a portentous half moon. Malachi is a kind-hearted boy. His long illness is forgotten.

Three years later, he dies. At the age of twenty-one, he is sucked into the spirals of the river on a dark night. The verdict at the inquest: death by accident. The pathologist does not fail to take note of Malachi's remarkable tongue, wide as two normal tongues, linked by a membrane of skin. It must have made breathing difficult in those final moments. Malachi's mother attends the inquest, too distraught to be called as a witness. Afterwards, in the car park, the tall man catches up to her. He is about her age. (He has blue eyes. Fine lines web the corners.) He is silent. The sun beats down, mid-July, a day that ridicules mourning. She is still a woman of some beauty.

"It would have happened long ago," she says, "But for a pact. Three years ago I made them agree to it. One voice was to be in command all day, then after dark the other would take over. They just shifted the patch. But the girl drove them against each other again. They were jealous over her. They couldn't share her any longer. They needed to fight it out. But there was only the one body to hurt."

She can no longer control herself. She sobs, and begs the man to leave her alone. A neighbour takes her by the arm to a waiting car. The man with blue eyes watches her go. He knows what must be done.

He drives to where the girl lives, a country motel, a run-down place, peeling green paint. She greets him solemnly, invites him up to her room. A lank-haired girl, not beautiful. He savours her quiet voice.

"He was a good friend to me," telling of Malachi, "I could trust him. On sunny days, we just sat by the river and talked. He said everything was under control. I was not to worry about his moods at night. I told him I liked him just as much at night when he switched the patch and changed his voice. At night, he would drink and drink, and make love. I told him how much I loved the feel of his tongue on my body. I suppose he didn't believe me."

She asks the man with the blue eyes to wait with her for a while. He stays, consoles her. It is dark when he leaves.

Ten years have passed. I am on an assignment to this country town. It is a pleasant summer's morning with, strangely, an arc of moon still visible in the bright sky like a single heel-print on glare ice. I am here to observe two children. They are twins, I am told. I am a little afraid of what I may find. I have a fear of children.

They don't look especially alike. One is fair, composed, the other dark and fidgety. They are ten years old. They speak in a babble no one has been able to understand. Aside from themselves, that is, for they seem to understand each other.

I am here with the other observers because of a curious development. The twins have discovered how to

communicate with the world. When they wish to be understood by others, we are told, they join hands and speak in
unison. The sounds blend together and produce words that
are intelligible.

The twins do not seem happy to meet our group of
linguists, philologists, semanticists, etymologists, cynics,
believers. Amongst us, the tall man with blue eyes. Fine lines
web the corners. He seems anxious.

At length the boys' mother, who has not changed much
over the years, asks them to speak to us. They hesitate, resolve
to please her. They join hands. The two solo voices that,
separately, are incomprehensible to the audience, blend together in a curious duet:

"Please help us, Father," they cry.

This evokes great delight on the part of the other observers.
They demand more. But the two little boys stand firm, hand-
in-hand. They look directly at me. They repeat, for me, their
shy, angry chant:

"Please help us, Father," they plead.

They are staring directly at the man with blue eyes. He
glances around fearfully, understands that the boys are making their appeal only to him. He looks at me in desperation.
He can no longer refuse to acknowledge me. I, for my part,
am ready to acknowledge him. I try to control my terror. I
extend my hand to him. I find I am alone. Alone, for the first
time, with my children.

The Distances: The Diary of
Alina Reyes
Julio Cortázar

Julio Cortázar

(Argentina, 1914-1984)

Julio Cortázar was born in Belgium of Argentinian parents. He grew up in Argentina but, as an adult, lived in Paris, where he wrote in Spanish.

He was greatly influenced by the works of le Comte de Lautréamont, the major precursor of surrealism. Both writers share a fascination with man's bestiality, delight in erotic imagery, describe grandiose hallucinations and gratuitious violence. In Cortázar's story "The Other Heaven" an Argentinian sees his double walking among the women of the night in Galerie Vivenne in Paris. When they meet, he challenges his double. "Those eyes don't belong to you ... Where did you get them?" The double is a strangler, Laurent, a short form of Lautréamont. The words quoted are from Lautréamont's *Chants de Maldoror* (1868).

Cortázar's work abounds in images of doubles and otherness. In "Axolotl," a man's psyche enters the body of an amphibian; in "Blow-Up" (the source of Antonioni's film), a photograph usurps the life of its photographer; and in "Continuity of Parks," a man is transformed into a character in the novel he is reading. Cortázar enlarges this last theme in his unique novel *Hopscotch* (1966)—actually two books—by urging the reader to enter the fiction.

In "The Distances," a woman is able to communicate with the "other" through a mysterious field transcending time and space. The reader will sense in this story what Gabriel Garcia Marquez found at the core of Cortázar: "something of the supernatural about it, tender and yet unfamiliar."

The Distances: The Diary of Alina Reyes

JANUARY 12

Last night it happened again, I so tired of bracelets and cajoleries, of pink champagne and Renato Viñes' face, oh that face like a spluttering seal, that picture of Dorian Gray in the last stages. It was a pleasure to go to bed to the *Red Bank Boogie*, with a chocolate mint, mama ashen-faced and yawning (as she always comes back from parties, ashen and half-asleep, an enormous fish and not even that).

Nora who says to fall asleep when it's light, the hubbub already starting in the street in the middle of the urgent chronicles her sister tells half-undressed. How happy they are, I turn off the lights and the hands, take all my clothes off to the cries of daytime and stirring, I want to sleep and I'm a terrible sounding bell, a wave, the chain the dog trails all night against the privet hedges. Now I lay me down to sleep ... I have to recite verses, or the system of looking for words with *a*, then with *a* and *e*, with five vowels, with four. With two and one consonant (obo, emu), with four consonants and a vowel (crass, dross), then the poems again, The moon came down to the forge/ in its crinoline of tuberoses./ The boy looks and looks./ The boy is looking at it. With three and three in alternate order, cabala, bolero, animal; pavane, Canada, repose, regale.

So hours pass: with four, with three and two, then later palindromes: easy ones like hah, bob, mom, did, dad, gag, radar; then more complicated or nice silly ones like oho Eve oho, or the Napoleon joke, "able was I ere I saw Elba." Or the beautiful anagrams: Salvador Dali, *avida dollars*; Alina Reyes, *es la reina y* . . . That one's so nice because it opens a path, because it does not close. Because the queen and . . . *la reina y* . . .

No, horrible, Horrible because it opens a path to this one who is not the queen and whom I hate again at night. To her who is Alina Reyes but not the queen of the anagram; let her be anything, a Budapest beggar, a beginner at a house of prostitution in Jujuy, a servant in Quetzaltenango, any place that's far away and not the queen. But yes Alina Reyes and because of that last night it happened again, to feel her and the hate.

JANUARY 20

At times I know that she's cold, that she suffers, that they beat her. I can only hate her so much, detest the hands that throw her to the ground and her as well, her even more because they beat her, because I am I and they beat her. Oh, I'm not so despondent when I'm sleeping or when I cut a suit or it's the hours mama receives and I'm serving tea to señora Regules or to the boy from the Rivas'. Then it's less important to me, it's a little more like something personal, I with myself; I feel she is more mistress of her adversity, far away and alone, but the mistress. Let her suffer, let her freeze; I endure it from here, and I believe that then I help her a little. Like making bandages for a soldier who hasn't been wounded yet, and to feel that's acceptable, that one is soothing him beforehand, providentially.

Let her suffer. I give a kiss to señora Regules, tea to the boy from the Rivas', and I keep myself for that inner resistance. I say to myself, "Now I'm crossing a bridge, it's all frozen, now the snow's coming in through my shoes. They're broken." It's not that she's feeling nothing. I only know it's like that, that on one side I'm crossing a bridge at the same instant (but I don't know if it is at the same instant) as the boy from the Rivas' accepts the cup of tea from me and puts on his best spoiled face. And I stand it all right because I'm alone among all these people without sensitivity and I'm not so despondent. Nora was petrified last night, and asked, "But what's happening to you?" It was happening to that one, to me far off. Something horrible must have happened to her, they were beating her or she was feeling sick and just when Nora was going to sing Fauré and I at the piano gazing happily at Luis María leaning with his elbows on the back of it which made him look like a model, he gazing at me with his puppy-look, the two of us so close and loving one another so much. It's worse when that happens, when I know something about her just at the moment I'm dancing with Luis María, kissing him, or just near him. Because in the distances they do not love me—her. That's the part they don't like and as it doesn't suit me to be rent to pieces inside and to feel they are beating me or that the snow is coming in through my shoes when Luis María is dancing with me and his hand on my waist makes the strong odor of oranges, or of cut hay, rise in me like heat at midday, and they are beating her and it's impossible to fight back, and I have to tell Luis María that I don't feel well, it's the humidity, humidity in all that snow which I do not feel, which I do not feel and it's coming in through my shoes.

JANUARY 25

Sure enough, Nora came to see me and made a scene. "Look, doll, that's the last time I ask you to play piano for me. We were quite an act." What did I know abut acts, I accompanied her as best I could, I remember hearing her as though she were muted. *Votre âme est un paysage choisi* ... but I watched my hands on the keys and it seemed to me they were playing all right, that they accompanied Nora decently. Luis María also was watching my hands. Poor thing, I think that was because it didn't cheer him up particularly to look at my face. I must look pretty strange.

Poor little Nora. Let someone else accompany her. (Each time this seems more of a punishment, now I know myself there only when I'm about to be happy, when I am happy, when Nora is singing Fauré I know myself there and only the hate is left.)

NIGHT

At times it's tenderness, a sudden and necessary tenderness toward her who is not queen and walks there. I would like to send her a telegram, my respects, to know that her sons are well or that she does not have sons—because I don't think there I have sons—and could use consolation, compassion, candy. Last night I fell asleep thinking up messages, places to meet. WILL ARRIVE THURSDAY STOP MEET ME AT BRIDGE. What bridge? An idea that recurs just as Budapest always recurs, to believe in the beggar in Budapest where they'll have lots of bridges and percolating snow. Then I sat straight up in bed and almost bawling, I almost run and wake mama, bite her to make her wake up. I keep on thinking about it. It is still not easy to say it. I keep on thinking that if I really wanted to, if it struck my fancy, I would be able to go to Budapest right away. Or to Jujuy or Quetzaltenango. (I went

back to look up those names, pages back.) Useless, it would
be the same as saying Tres Arroyos, Kobe, Florida Street in the
400-block. Budapest just stays because *there* it's cold, there
they beat me and abuse me. There (I dreamed it, it's only a
dream, but as it sticks and works itself into my wakefulness)
there's someone called Rod—or Erod, or Rodo—and he beats
me and I love him, I don't know if I love him but I let him
beat me, that comes back day after day, so I guess I do love
him.

LATER

A lie. I dreamed of Rod or made him from some dream figure
already worn out or to hand. There's no Rod, they're punish-
ing me there, but who knows whether it's a man, an angry
mother, a solitude.

Come find me. To say to Luis María, "We're getting married and you're taking me to Budapest, to a bridge where
there's snow and someone." I say: and if I am? (Because I
think all that from the secret vantage point of not seriously
believing it. And if I am?) All right, if I am ... But plain
crazy, plain. . . ? What a honeymoon!

JANUARY 28

I thought of something odd. It's been three days now that
nothing has come to me from the distances. Maybe they don't
beat her now, or she could have come by a coat. To send her a
telegram, some stockings ... I thought of something odd. I
arrived in the terrible city and it was afternoon, a green
watery afternoon as afternoons never are if one does not help
out by thinking of them. Beside the Dobrina Stana, on the
Skorda Prospect equestrian statues bristling with stalagmites
of hoarfrost and stiff policemen, great smoking loaves of
coarse bread and flounces of wind puffing in the windows. At

a tourist's pace, walking by the Dobrina, the map in the pocket of my blue suit (in this freezing weather and to leave my coat in the Burglos), until I come to a plaza next to the river, nearly in the river thundering with broken ice floes and barges and some kingfisher which is called there *sbunáia tjèno* or something worse.

I supposed that the bridge came after the plaza. I thought that and did not want to go on. It was the afternoon of Elsa Piaggio de Tarelli's concert at the Odeón, I fussed over getting dressed, unwilling, suspecting that afterwards only insomnia would be waiting for me. This thought of the night, so much of night . . . Who knows if I would not get lost. One invents names while traveling, thinking, remembers them at the moment: Dobrina Stana, *sbunáia tjéno*, the Burglos. But I don't know the name of the square, it is a little as though one had really walked into a plaza in Budapest and was lost because one did not know its name; if there's no name, how can there be a plaza?

I'm coming, mama. We'll get to your Bach all right, and your Brahms. The way there is easy. No plaza, no Hotel Burglos. We are here, Elsa Piaggio there. Sad to have to interrupt this, to know that I'm in a plaza (but that's not sure yet, I only think so and that's nothing, less than nothing). And that at the end of the plaza the bridge begins.

NIGHT

Begins, goes on. Between the end of the concert and the first piece I found the name and the route. Vladas Square and the Market Bridge. I crossed Vladas Square to where the bridge started, going along slowly and wanting to stop at times, to stay in the houses or store windows, in small boys all bundled up and the fountains with tall heroes with their long cloaks all white, Tadeo Alanko and Vladislas Néroy, tokay drinkers and cymbalists. I saw Elsa Piaggio acclaimed between one

Chopin and another Chopin, poor thing, and my orchestra seat gave directly onto the plaza, with the beginning of the bridge between the most immense columns. But I was thinking this, notice, it's the same as making the anagram *es la reina y* . . . in place of Alina Reyes, or imagining mama at the Suarez's house instead of beside me. Better not to fall for that nonsense; that's something very strictly my own, to give in to the desire, the real desire. Real because Alina, well, let's go— Not the other thing, not feeling her being cold or that they mistreat her. I long for this and follow it by choice, by knowing where it's going, to find out if Luis María is going to take me to Budapest. Easier to go out and look for that bridge, to go out on my own search and find myself, as now, because now I've walked to the middle of the bridge amid shouts and applause, between "Albéniz!" and more applause and "The Polonaise!" as if that had any meaning amid the whipping snow which pushes against my back with the wind-force, hands like a thick towel around my waist drawing me to the center of the bridge.

(It's more convenient to speak in the present tense. This was at eight o'clock when Elsa Piaggio was playing the third piece, I think it was Julián Aguirre or Carlos Guastavino, something with pastures and little birds.) I have grown coarse with time, I have no respect for her now. I remember I thought one day: "There they beat me, there the snow comes in through my shoes and I know it at that moment, when it is happening to me there I know it at the same time. But why at the same time? Probably I'm coming late, probably it hasn't happened yet. Probably they will beat her within fourteen years or she's already a cross and an epitaph in the Sainte-Ursule cemetery." And that seemed to me pleasant, possible, quite idiotic. Because behind that, one falls always into the matching time. If now she were really starting over the bridge, I know I would feel it myself, from here. I remember that I stopped to look at the river which was like spoiled mayonnaise thrashing against the abutments, furiously as possible, noisy and lashing. (This last I was thinking.) It was worth it to lean over the parapet of the bridge and to hear in my ears the grinding of the ice there below. It was worth it to stop a little bit for the view, a little bit from fear too which came from inside—or it was being without a coat, the light snowfall melting and my topcoat at the hotel—And after all, for I am an unassuming girl, a girl without petty prides, but let them come tell me that the same thing could have happened to anyone else, that she could have journeyed to Hungary in the middle of the Odeón. Say, that would give anyone the shivers!

But mama was pulling at my sleeve, there was hardly anyone left in the orchestra section. I'm writing to that point, not wishing to go on remembering what I thought. I'm going to get sick if I go on remembering. But it's certain, certain; I thought of an odd thing.

JANUARY 30

Poor Luis María, what an idiot to get married to me. He doesn't know what he'll get on top of that. Or underneath that, Nora says, posing as an emancipated intellectual.

JANUARY 31

We'll be going there. He was so agreeable about it I almost screamed. I was afraid, it seemed to me that he entered into this game too easily. And he doesn't know anything, he's like a queen's pawn that sews up the game without even suspecting it. The little pawn Luis María beside his queen. Beside the queen and—

FEBRUARY 7

What's important now is to get better. I won't write the end of what I had thought at the concert. Last night again I sensed her suffering. I know that they're beating me there again. I can't avoid knowing it, but enough chronicle. If I had limited myself to setting this down regularly just as a whim, as alleviation . . . It was worse, a desire to understand in reading it over; to find keys in each word set to paper after those nights. Like when I thought of the plaza, the torn river and the noises and afterwards . . . But I'm not writing that, I'll never, ever, write that.

To go there to convince myself that celibacy has been no good for me, that it's nothing more than that, to be twenty-seven years old and never to have had a man. Now he will be my puppy, my penguin, enough to think and to be, to be finally and for good.

Nevertheless, now that I shall close this diary, for one gets married or one keeps a diary, the two things don't go well together—even now I don't want to finish it up without saying this with the happiness of hope, with hope for happiness. We will go there but it doesn't have to be what I thought the night of the concert. (I'll write it, and enough of the diary as far as I'm concerned.) I will find her on the bridge and we will look at one another. The night of the concert I felt echo in my ears the grinding of the ice there below. And it will be the queen's victory over that malignant relationship, that soundless and unlawful encroachment. If I am really I, she will yield, she will join my radiant *zone*, my lovelier and surer life; I have only to go to her side and lay a hand on her shoulder.

Alina Reyes de Aráoz and her husband arrived in Budapest April sixth, and took accommodations at the Ritz. That was two months before their divorce. On the afternoon of the second day, Alina went out to get to know the city and enjoy the thaw. As it pleased her to walk alone—she was brisk and curious—she went in twenty different directions looking vaguely for something, but without thinking about it too much, content to let her desire choose, that it express itself in abrupt changes of direction which led her from one store window to another, crossing streets, moving from one showcase to another.

She came to the bridge and crossed it as far as the middle, walking now with some difficulty because the snow hindered her and from the Danube a wind comes up from below, a difficult wind which hooks and lashes. She felt as though her skirt were glued to her thighs (she was not dressed properly for the weather) and suddenly a desire to turn around, to go back to the familiar city. At the center of the desolate bridge the ragged woman with black straight hair waited with something fixed and anxious in the lined face, in the folding of the hands, a little closed but already outstretched. Alina was close to her, repeating, now she knew, facial expressions and distances as if after a dress rehearsal. Without foreboding, liberating herself at last—she believed it in one terrible, jubilant, cold leap—she was beside her and also stretched out her hands, refusing to think, and the woman on the bridge hugged her against her chest and the two, stiff and silent, embraced one another on the bridge with the crumbling river hammering against the abutments.

Alina ached: it was the clasp of the pocketbook, the strength of the embrace had run it in between her breasts with a sweet, bearable laceration. She surrounded the slender woman feeling her complete and absolute within her arms, with a springing up of happiness equal to a hymn, to loosing a cloud of pigeons, to the river singing. She shut her eyes in the total fusion, declining the sensations from outside, the evening light; suddenly very tired but sure of her victory, without celebrating it so much as her own and at last.

It seemed to her that one of the two of them was weeping softly. It should have been her because she felt her cheeks wet, and even the cheekbone aching as though she had been struck there. Also the throat, and then suddenly the shoulders,

weighed down by innumerable hardships. Opening her eyes
(perhaps now she screamed) she saw that they had separated.
Now she did scream. From the cold, because the snow was
coming in through her broken shoes, because making her
way along the roadway to the plaza went Alina Reyes, very
lovely in her grey suit, her hair a little loose against the wind,
not turning her face. Going off.

Translated from the Spanish by Paul Blackburn

Two in One
Algernon Blackwood

Algernon Blackwood

(England, 1869-1951)

Algernon Blackwood, the "Master of Horror," recalled in his autobiography, *Episodes Before Thirty* (1923), "I loved the night, the
shadows, empty rooms and haunted wood," and it was these that
moved him to write his enthralling stories of that shadowy "other"
world beyond.

After a sheltered childhood, Blackwood departed for Canada at
his father's suggestion in 1890. In Toronto, he worked for an
insurance company and became a founding member of Madame
Blavatsky's Theosophical Society. When his money ran out, he
escaped to Muskoka and spent several months on Bohemia Island,
north of Port Carling, living an enchanted life away from the
business world. This stay inspired his first short story, "A Haunted
Island." A move to New York followed, where after a period of
poverty and drug taking, he joined *The New York Times* as a
reporter. Yearning for London, Blackwood returned to England in
1899 and began writing in earnest. His first collection, *The Empty
House and Other Ghost Stories* (1906), received praise from Hilaire
Belloc, and two years later his detective collection, *John Silence,
Physician Extraordinary*, won him a wide readership.

Blackwood, like the protagonist Le Maître in "Two in One," was
a solitary, philosophically detached spinner of successful yarns.
Late in life he became known to thousands as "the Ghost Man,"
presenting his stories and experiences before the microphone and
camera. He won the Television Society's medal in 1948, and was
awarded a CBE (Commander of the British Empire) the following
year.

Two in One

Some idle talker, playing with half-truths, had once told him that he was too self-centred to fall in love—out of himself; he was unwilling to lose himself in another; and that was the reason he had never married. But Le Maître was not really more of an egoist than is necessary to make a useful man. A too selfless person is ever ineffective. The suggestion, nevertheless, had remained to distress, for he was no great philosopher—merely a writer of successful tales—tales of wild Nature chiefly; the "human interest" (a publisher's term) was weak; the great divine enigma of an undeveloped soul—certainly of a lover's or a woman's soul—had never claimed his attention enough, perhaps. He was somewhat too much detached from human life. Nature had laid so powerful a spell upon his heart. . . .

"I hope she won't be late," ran the practical thought across his mind as he waited that early Sunday morning in the Great Central Station and reflected that it was the cleanest, brightest, and most airy terminus of all London. He had promised her the whole day out—a promise somewhat long neglected.

He was not conscious of doing an unselfish act, yet on the whole, probably, he would rather—or just as soon—have been alone.

The air was fragrant, and the sunshine blazed in soft white patches on the line. The maddening loveliness of an exceptional spring danced everywhere into his heart. Yes, he rather wished he were going off into the fields and woods alone, instead of with her. Only—she was really a dear person, more, far more now, than secretary and typist; more, even, than the devoted girl who had nursed him through that illness. A friend she was; the years of their working together had made her that; and she was wise and gentle. Oh, yes; it would be delightful to have her with him. How she would enjoy the long sunny day.

Then he saw her coming toward him through the station. In a patch of sunshine she came, as though the light produced her—came suddenly from the middle of a group of men in flannels carrying golf-sticks. And he smiled his welcome a little paternally, trying to kill the selfish though that he would rather have been alone. Soft things fluttered about her. The big hat was becoming. She was dressed in brown, he believed.

He bought a Sunday paper. "I must buy one too," she laughed. She chose one with pictures, chose it at random rather. He had never heard its name even. And in a first-class carriage alone—he meant to do it really well—they raced through a world of sunshine and brilliant fields to Amersham. She was very happy. She tried every seat in turn; the blazing sheets of yellow—such a spring for buttercups there had never been—drew her from side to side. She put her head out, and nearly lost her big hat, and that soft fluttering thing she wore streamed behind her like the colour of escaping flowers. She opened both windows. The very carriage held the perfume of May that floated over the whole country-side.

He was very nice to her, but read his paper—though always

ready with a smile and answer when she asked for them. She teased and laughed and chattered. The luncheon packages engaged her serious attention. Never for a moment was she still, trying every corner in turn, putting her feet up, and bouncing to enjoy the softness of the first-class cushions. "You'll be sitting in the rack next," he suggested. But her head was out of the window again and she did not hear him. She was radiant as a child. His paper interested him—book reviews or something. "I've asked you that three times, you know, already," he heard her laughing opposite. And with a touch of shame he tossed the paper through the window. "There! I'd quite forgotten her again!" he thought, with a touch of shame. "I must pull myself together." For it was true. He had for the moment—more than once—forgotten her existence, just as though he really were alone.

Together they strolled down through the beech-wood toward Amersham, he for ever dropping the luncheon packages, which she picked up again and tried to stuff into his pockets. For she refused to carry anything at all. "It's *my* day out, not yours, remember! *I* do no work to-day!" And he caught her happiness, pausing to watch her while she picked flowers and leaves and all the rest, and disentangling without the least impatience that soft fluttering thing she wore when it caught in thorns, and even talking with her about this wild spring glory as though she were just the companion that he needed out of all the world. He no longer felt quite so conscious of her objective presence as at first. In the train, for instance, he had felt so vividly aware that she was there. Alternately he had forgotten and remembered her presence. Now it was better. They were more together, as it were. "I wish I were alone," he thought once more as the beauty of the spring called to him tumultuously and he longed to lie and dream it all, unhampered by another's presence. Then, even while thinking it, realized that he was—alone. It was curious.

This happened even in their first wood when they went downhill into Amersham. As they left it and passed again into the open it came. And on its heels, as he watched her moving here and there light-footed as a child or nymph, there came this other instinctive thought—"I wish I were ten years younger than I am!"—the first time in all his life, probably, that such a thought had ever bothered him. Apparently he said it aloud, laughingly, as he watched her dancing movements. For she turned and ran up to his side quickly, her little face quite grave beneath the big hat's rim. "You *are!*" That answer struck him as rather wonderful. Who was she after all . . . ?

And in Amersham they hired from the Griffin a rickety old cart, drawn by a still more rickety horse, to drive them to Penn's Wood. She, with her own money, bought stone-bottle ginger-beer—two bottles. It made her day complete to have those bottles, though unless they had driven she would have done without them. The street was deserted, drenched in blazing sunshine. Rooks were cawing in the elms behind the church. Not a soul was about as they crawled away from the houses and passed upward between hedges smothered in cow-parsley over the hill. She had kept her picture paper. It lay on her lap all the way. She never opened it or turned a single page; but she held it in her lap. They drove in silence. The old man on the box was like a faded, weather-beaten farmer dressed in somebody else's cast-off Sunday coat. He flicked the horse with a tattered whip. Sometimes he grunted. Plover rose from the fields, cuckoos called, butterflies danced sideways past the carriage, eyeing them . . . and, as they passed through Penn Street, Le Maître started suddenly and said something. For, again, he had quite forgotten she was there. "What a selfish beast I am! Why can't I forget myself and my own feelings, and look after her and make her feel amused and happy? It's *her* day out, not mine!" This, somehow, was the way he put it to himself, just as an ordinary man would have put it. But, when he turned to look at her, he received a shock. Here was something new and unexpected. With a thud it dropped down into his mind—crash!

For at the sound of his voice she looked up confused and startled into his face. She had forgotten *him*! For the first time in all the years together—years of work, of semi-official attention to his least desire, yet of personal devotion as well, because she respected him and thought him wonderful—she had forgotten *he* was there. She had forgotten his existence beside her as a separate person. She, too, had been—alone.

It was here, perhaps, he first realized this singular thing that set this day apart from every other day that he had ever known. In reality, of course, it had come far sooner—begun with the exquisite spring dawn before either of them was awake, had tentatively fluttered about his soul even while he stood waiting for her in the station, come softly nearer all the way in the train, dropped threads of its golden web about him, especially in that first beech-wood, then moved with its swifter yet unhurried rush—until, here, now, in this startling moment, he realized it fully. Thus steal those changes o'er the sky, perhaps, that the day itself knows at sunrise, but that unobservant folk do not notice till the sun bursts out with fuller explanation, and they say, "The weather's changed; how delightful! how unexpected!" Le Maître had never been very observant—of people.

And then in this deep, lonely valley, too full of sunshine to hold anything else, it seemed, they stopped where the beech-woods trooped to the edge of the white road. No wind was here; it was still and silent; the leaves glittered, motionless. They entered the thick trees together, she carrying the ginger-beer bottles *and* that picture paper. He noticed that: the way she held it, almost clutched it, still unopened. Her face, he saw, was pale. Or was it merely the contrast of the shade? The trees were very big and wonderful. No birds sang; the network of dazzling sunshine-patches in the gloom bewildered a little.

At first they did not talk at all, and then in hushed voices. But it was only when they were some way into the wood, and she had put down the bottles—though not the paper—to pick a flower or spray of leaves, that he traced the singular secret thrill to its source and understood why he had felt—no, not uneasy, but so strangely moved. For he had asked the sleepy driver of the way, and how they might best reach Beaconsfield across Penn's Wood, and the old man's mumbled answer took no note of—her.

"It's a bit rough, maybe, on t'other side, stony-like and steep, but that ain't nothing for a gentleman—when he's alone . . . !"

The words disturbed him with a sense of darkness, yet of wonder. As though the old man had not noticed her; almost as though he had seen only one person—himself. . . .

They lunched among heather and bracken just beside a pool of sunshine. In front lay a copse of pines, with little beeches in between. The roof was thick just there, the stillness haunting. All the country-side, it seemed, this Sunday noon, had gone to sleep, he and she alone left out of the deep, soft dream. He watched those pines, mothering the slim young beeches, the brilliant fresh greens of whose lower branches, he thought, were like little platforms of level sunlight amid the general gloom—patches that had left the ground to escape by the upper air and had then been caught.

"Look," he heard, "they make one think of laughter crept in unawares among a lot of solemn monks—or of children lost among grave elder beings whose ways are dull and sombre!" It was his own thought continued . . . yet it was she, lying there beside him, who had said it. . . .

And all that wonderful afternoon she had this curious way of picking the thoughts out of his mind and putting them into words for him. "Look," she said again later, "you can always tell whether the wind loves a tree or not by the way it blows the branches. If it loves them, it tries to draw them out to go away with it. The others it merely shakes carelessly as it passes!" It was the very thought in his own mind, too. Indeed, he had been on the point of saying it, but had desisted, feeling she would not understand, with the half-wish—though far less strong than before—that he were alone to enjoy it all in his own indulgent way. Then, even more swiftly, came that other strange sensation that he *was* alone all the time; more—that he was for the first time in his life most wonderfully complete and happy, all sense of isolation gone.

He turned quickly the instant she had said it. But not quickly enough. By the look in her grey eyes, by the expression on the face where the discarded hat no longer hid it, he read the amazing enigma he had half divined before. She, too, was alone. She had forgotten him again—forgotten his presence—radiant and happy without him, enjoying herself in her own way. She had merely uttered her delightful thoughts aloud, as if speaking to herself!

How the afternoon, with its long sunny hours, passed so quickly away, he never understood, nor how they made their way eventually to Beaconsfield through other woods and over other meadows. He remembers only that the whole time he kept forgetting that she was with him, and then suddenly remembering it again. And once on the grass, when they rested to drink the cold tea from his rather musty flask, he lit his pipe, and after a bit he—dozed. He actually slept; for ten minutes at her side, yes, he slept. He heard her laughing at him, but the laughter was faint and very far away; it might just as well have been the wind in the cow-parsley that said, "If you sleep, I shall change you—change you while you sleep!" And for some minutes after he woke again it hardly seemed queer to him that he did not see her, for when he noticed her coming toward him from the hedgerow, her arms full of flowers and things, he only thought, "Oh, there she is" —as though her absence, or his own absence in sleep, were not quite the common absences of the world.

And he remembered that on the walk to the village her shoe hurt her, and he offered to carry her, and that then she took her shoe off and ran along the grass beside the lane the whole way. But it was at the inn where they had their supper that the oddest thing of all occurred, for the deaf and rather stupid servant-girl would insist on laying the table on the lawn for —one.

"Oh, expectin' someone, are yer?" she said at last. "Is that it?" and so brought plates and knives for two. The girl never once looked at his companion—almost as though she did not see her and seemed unaware of her presence. Le Maître began to feel that he was dreaming. This was a dream-country, where the people had curious sight. He remembered the driver. . . .

In the dusk they made their way to the station. They spoke no word. He kept losing sight of her. Once or twice he forgot who he was. But the whole amazing thing blazed into him most strongly, showing how it had seized upon his mind, when he stood before the ticket-window and hesitated—for a second—how many tickets he should buy. He stammered at length for two first-class, but he was absurdly flustered for a second. It had actually occurred to him that they needed only one ticket. . . .

And suddenly in the train he understood—and his heart came up in his throat. They were alone. He turned to her where she lay in the corner, feet up, weary, crumpled among the leaves and flowers she had gathered. Like a hedgerow flower she looked, tired by the sunshine and the wind. In one hand was the picture paper, still unopened and unread, sym-bol of everyday reality. She was dozing certainly, if not actually asleep. So he woke her with a touch, calling her name aloud.

There were no words at first. He looked at her, coming up very close to do so, and she looked back at him—straight into his eyes—just as she did at home when they were working and he was explaining something important. And then her own eyes dropped, and a deep blush spread over all her face.

"I wasn't asleep—really," she said, as he took her at last into his arms; "I was wondering—when—you'd find out."

"Come to myself, you mean?" he asked tremblingly.

"Well," she hesitated, as soon as she got breath, "that I *am* yourself—and that you are me. Of course, we're really only one. I knew it years—oh, years and years ago. . . ."

In Memory of Pauline
Adolfo Bioy Casares

Adolfo Bioy Casares

(Argentina, b. 1914)

Adolfo Bioy Casares is a writer of novels, short stories and essays, whose work is frequently compared to that of Jorge Luis Borges. They share a preoccupation with labyrinths, doubles, and metaphysical puzzles. Close friends, Bioy and Borges began collaborating in the early 1940s, publishing their joint creations under the pseudonym Honorio Bustos Domecq. As Emir Rodriguez Monegal observed in his biography of Borges: "A new writer had been born, a writer who ought to be called 'Biorges' because he was neither Borges nor Bioy." Borges himself noted, "We have somehow begotten a third person that is quite unlike us." Domecq's first book was the *Six Problems of Don Isidro Parodi*, a fantastic parody of the classic detective story. *The Chronicles of Bustos Domecq* followed, a collection of outrageous, often hilarious parodies of literary and artistic life.

Despite this collaboration, one perhaps sees more of Bioy in Domecq's works than of Borges. In Bioy's "The Invention of Morel" a man falls in love with a holograph. This story is said to have inspired the film *Last Year at Marienbad*, and certainly Bioy's tales possess a similar elegant, dreamlike quality. In "The Celestial Plot," a pilot takes off from one Buenos Aires and lands at another; in *The Dream of Heroes*, a man lives the same carnival night twice, experiencing different versions of the same reality.

In Borges's "Tlön, Uqbar, Orbis Tertius," the character Bioy states that "mirrors and copulation are abominable, because they increase the number of men." "In Memory of Pauline" suggests something of this horror, when the protagonist's lover returns to him through the "mirror" of another man's mind.

In Memory of Pauline

I always loved Pauline. One of my earliest memories is of the day when Pauline and I were hiding under a leafy bower of laurel branches in a garden with two stone lions. Pauline said, "I like blue, I like grapes, I like ice, I like roses, I like white horses." I knew then that my happiness had begun, for in those preferences I could identify myself with Pauline. We resembled each other so miraculously that in the book about the final union of souls with the soul of the world, she wrote in the margin: "Ours have already been united." At that time *ours* meant her soul and mine.

To explain that similarity I argued that I was a hasty and imperfect copy, a rough draft of Pauline. I remember that I wrote in my notebook: "Every poem is a copy of Poetry and in each thing there is a prefiguration of God." Then I thought: My resemblance to Pauline is what saves me. I saw (and even now I see) that my identification with her was the best influence on my life, a kind of sanctuary where I would be purged of my natural defects: apathy, negligence, vanity.

Life was a pleasant habit which led us to look upon our

eventual marriage as something natural and certain. Pauline's parents, unimpressed by the literary prestige that I prematurely won and lost, promised to give their consent when I received my doctorate. And many times we imagined an orderly future with enough time to work, to travel, and to love each other. We imagined it so vividly, we were convinced that it could not fail to come true.

Although we spoke of marriage, we did not regard each other as sweethearts. We had spent our whole childhood together, and we continued to treat each other with the shy reticence of children. I did not dare to play the role of a lover and tell her solemnly, "I love you." But still I did love her, I was mad about her, and my startled and scrupulous eyes were dazzled by her perfection.

Pauline liked me to entertain friends. She always made the preparations, attended to the guests, and, secretly, pretended to be the mistress of the house. But I must confess that I did not enjoy those affairs. The party we gave to introduce Julius Montero to some writers was no exception.

The night before, Montero had visited me for the first time. He came in brandishing a voluminous manuscript which he, with an air of a tyrant, read to me in its entirety, secure in his belief that an unpublished literary work conferred on its author the right to usurp as much of another person's time as he desired. Soon after he left I had already forgotten his swarthy, unshaven face. The only interesting thing about the story he read me—Montero urged me to tell him quite honestly whether it had too strong an impact—was that it seemed to be a vague attempt to imitate a number of completely different writers. The theme of the story was that if a certain melody issues from a relationship between the violin and the movements of the violinist, then the soul of each person issues from a definite relationship between movement and matter. The hero made a machine—a kind of frame, with pieces of wood and ropes—to produce souls. Then he died.

There was a wake and a burial, but he was secretly alive in the frame. At the end of the story the frame appeared near a stereoscope and a Galena stone supported by a tripod in the room where a young girl had died.

When I managed to change the subject, Montero expressed a strange desire to meet some writers.

"Why don't you come over tomorrow afternoon?" I suggested. "I'll introduce you to some."

He described himself as a savage and accepted the invitation. Perhaps my pleasure in seeing him leave was what induced me to accompany him to the street floor. When we left the elevator, Montero discovered the garden out in the courtyard. Sometimes, when seen through the glass door from the hall in the thin afternoon light, that tiny garden suggests the mysterious image of a forest at the bottom of a lake. At night the glow of lilac and orange lights changes it into a horrible candyland paradise. Montero saw it at night.

"To be frank with you," he said, after taking a long look, "this is the most interesting thing I have seen here so far."

The next day Pauline arrived early. By five that afternoon she had everything ready for the party. I showed her a Chinese figurine of jade which I had bought that morning in an antique shop. It was a wild horse with raised forefeet and a flowing mane. The shopkeeper had assured me that it symbolized passion.

Putting the little horse on a shelf of the bookcase, Pauline exclaimed, "It is beautiful, like a first love affair!" When I said I wanted her to have it, she threw her arms around my neck and kissed me impulsively.

We drank a cup of tea together. I told her I had been offered a fellowship to study in London for two years. Suddenly we believed in an immediate marriage, the trip to England, our life there. We considered details of domestic economy: the almost enjoyable privations we would suffer; the distribution of hours of study, diversion, rest, and, perhaps, work; what

Pauline would do while I attended classes; the clothes and books we would take. And then, after an interval of planning, we conceded that I would have to give up the scholarship. My examinations were only a week away, but already it was evident that Pauline's parents wished to postpone our marriage.

The guests began to arrive. I was not happy. I found it hard to talk to anyone, and kept inventing excuses to leave the room. I was in no mood for conversation; and I discovered that my memory was vague and unpredictable. Uneasy, futile, miserable, I moved from one group to another, wishing that people would leave, waiting for my moments alone with Pauline, while I escorted her home.

She was standing by the window, talking to Montero. When I glanced at her, she looked up and turned her perfect face toward me. I felt that her love was an inviolable refuge where we two were alone. Now I desired fervently to tell her that I adored her, and I made up my mind to abandon, that very evening, the absurd and childish reticence that had kept me, until then, from declaring my love. But if only I could communicate my thought to her without speaking! Her face wore an expression of generous, ecstatic, and surprised gratitude.

I walked over to Pauline, and she asked me the name of the poem in which a man becomes so estranged from a woman that he does not even greet her when they meet in heaven. I knew that the poem was by Browning, and I remembered some of the verses. I spent the rest of the evening looking for it in the Oxford Edition. If I could not have Pauline to myself, then I preferred to look for something she wanted instead of talking to people who did not interest me; but my mind was not functioning clearly, and I wondered if my lack of success in finding the poem was a kind of omen. When I turned toward the window again, they were gone. Louis Albert Morgan, the pianist, must have noticed my concern.

"Pauline is just showing Montero around the apartment," he said.

I shrugged my shoulders, tried to conceal my annoyance, and pretended to be interested in the Browning again. Out of the corner of my eye I caught a glimpse of Morgan entering my bedroom. I thought, "He has gone to find her." He came out, followed by Pauline and Montero.

Finally someone went home; then, slowly and deliberately, the others left. The moment came when no one was there except Pauline, Montero, and me. As I had feared, Pauline said, "It's very late. I have to go."

"I'll take you home, if I may," Montero volunteered quickly.

"So will I," I said.

I was speaking to Pauline, but I looked at Montero, and my eyes were filled with scorn and loathing.

When we came out of the elevator, I noticed that Pauline did not have the little Chinese horse I had given her.

"You've forgotten my present!" I said.

I went back to the apartment and returned with the figurine. I found them leaning against the glass door, looking at the garden. I took Pauline's arm and tried to keep Montero from walking on the other side of her. I very pointedly left him out of the conversation.

He was not offended. When we said good night to Pauline, he insisted on walking home with me. On the way he spoke of literature, probably with sincerity and with a certain favor. I said to myself, "He is the writer. I am just a tired man who is worried about a woman." I pondered on the incongruity between his physical vigor and his literary weakness. I thought, "He is protected by a hard shell. My feelings do not reach him." I looked with aversion at his clear eyes, his hairy moustache, his bull neck.

That week I scarcely saw Pauline. I studied a great deal. After my last examination I telephoned her. She

congratulated me with unnatural vehemence, and said she
would come to see me later that afternoon.

I took a nap, bathed slowly, and waited for Pauline while I
leafed through a book about the Fausts of Müller and Less-
ing.

When I saw her I exclaimed, "You've changed!"

"Yes," she said. "How well we know each other. You can
tell what I am thinking even before I speak."

Enraptured, we gazed into each other's eyes.

"Thank you," I said.

Nothing had ever touched me as much as that admission,
by Pauline, of the deep conformity of our souls. I basked
naively in the warmth of that compliment. I do not remember
when I began to wonder (incredulously) whether Pauline's
words had another meaning. Before I had time to consider
that possibility, she began a confused explanation.

Suddenly I heard her say, ". . . and that first afternoon we
were already hopelessly in love."

I wondered what she was talking about.

"He is very jealous," Pauline continued. "He doesn't object
to our friendship, but I promised that I wouldn't see you any
more for a while."

I was still waiting for the impossible clarification that
would reassure me. I did not know whether Pauline was
joking or serious. I did not know what sort of expression was
on my face. Nor did I know then the extent of my grief.

"I must go now," said Pauline. "Julius is waiting for me
downstairs. He didn't want to come up."

"Who?" I asked.

Suddenly, as if nothing had happened, I was afraid Pauline
had discovered that I was an impostor, and that she knew our
souls were not really united after all.

"Julius Montero," she answered ingenuously.

Her reply could not have surprised me; but on that horrible
afternoon nothing impressed me as much as those two words.

For the first time in my life I felt that a breach had opened between us.

"Are you going to marry him?" I asked almost scornfully.

I do not remember what she said. I believe she invited me to the wedding.

Then I was alone. The whole thing was absurd. No person was more incompatible with Pauline (and with me) than Montero. Or was I mistaken? If Pauline loved that man, perhaps she and I had never been alike at all. And as I came to that realization I was aware that I had suspected the dreadful truth many times before.

I was very sad, but I do not believe I was jealous. Lying face downward on my bed, I stretched out my arm and my hand touched the book I had been reading a short while before. I flung it away in disgust.

I went out for a walk. I stopped to watch a group of children playing at the corner. That afternoon, I did not see how I could go on living.

I could not forget Pauline. As I preferred the painful moments of our separation to my subsequent loneliness, I went over them and examined them in minute detail and relived them. As a result of my brooding anxiety, I thought I discovered new interpretations for what had happened. So, for example, in Pauline's voice telling me the name of her lover I found a tenderness that moved me deeply, at first. I thought that she was sorry for me, and her kindness was as touching as her love had been before. But then, after thinking it over, I decided that her tenderness was not meant for me but for the name she pronounced.

I accepted the followship, and quietly started to make preparations for the voyage. But the news got out. Pauline visited me the afternoon before I sailed.

I had felt alienated from her, but the moment I saw her I fell in love all over again. I realized that her visit was a clandestine one, although she did not say it. I grasped her hands. I trembled with gratitude.

"I shall always love you," said Pauline. "Somehow, I shall always love you more than anyone else."

Perhaps she thought she had committed an act of treason. She knew that I did not doubt her loyalty to Montero, but as if it troubled her to have spoken words that implied—if not for me, for an imaginary witness—a disloyal intention, she hastened to add, "Of course, what I feel for you doesn't count now. I am in love with Julius."

Nothing else mattered, she said. The past was a desert where she had waited for Montero. Of our love, or friendship, she had no memory.

There was not much to say after that. I was very angry, and pretended that I was busy. I took her down in the elevator. When I opened the door to the street, we saw that it was raining.

"I'll get you a taxi," I said.

But in a voice full of emotion Pauline shouted, "Good-bye, Darling!"

Then she ran across the street and was gone. I turned away sadly. When I looked around, I saw a man crouching in the garden. He stood up and pressed his face and hands against the glass door. It was Montero.

Streaks of lilac and orange-colored light were outlined against a green background of dark clumps of shrubbery. Montero's face, pressed against the wet glass, looked whitish and deformed.

I thought of an aquarium, of a fish in an aquarium. Then, with futile bitterness, I told myself that Montero's face suggested other monsters: the fish misshapen by the pressure of the water, living at the bottom of the sea.

I sailed the next morning. During the crossing I scarcely left my cabin. I wrote and studied constantly.

I wanted to forget Pauline. During my two years in England I avoided anything that could remind me of her, from encounters with other Argentines to the few dispatches from Buenos Aires published by the newspapers. It is true that she appeared to me in dreams with such persuasive and vivid reality that I wondered whether my soul was counteracting by night the privations I imposed on it during the day. I eluded the memory of her obstinately. By the end of the first year I succeeded in excluding her from my nights and, almost, in forgetting her.

The afternoon of my arrival from Europe I thought about Pauline again. I wondered whether the memories at my apartment would be too intense. When I opened the door I felt some emotion, and I paused respectfully to commemorate the past and the extremes of joy and sorrow I had known. Then I had a shameful revelation. I was not moved by the secret monuments of our love, suddenly bared in the depths of my memory: I was moved by the emphatic light streaming through the window, the light of Buenos Aires.

Around four o'clock I went to the corner store and bought a pound of coffee. At the bakery the clerk recognized me. He greeted me with noisy cordiality, and told me that for a long time—six months, at least—I had not honored him with my patronage. After those amenities I asked him timidly, foolishly, for a small loaf of bread. He asked the usual question, "White or dark?"

I replied, as usual, "White."

I went home. The day was clear and very cold.

I thought about Pauline while I was making coffee. Sometimes, late in the afternoon, we would drink a cup of black coffee together.

Then, as if I were in a dream, I shifted abruptly from my affable and even-tempered indifference to the excitement, the madness that the sight of Pauline caused me to feel. When I saw her, I fell down on my knees, I buried my face in her hands and, for the first time, I gave vent to all my grief at having lost her.

It happened this way: I heard three knocks at the door. I wondered who it was: I remembered that my coffee would get cold; I opened the door with a certain irritation.

And then—I do not know how long all this took—Pauline asked me to follow her. I realized that she was correcting, by her forceful actions, the mistakes of our past relationship. It seems to me (but I tend to be inaccurate about that afternoon) that she corrected them with excessive determination. When she asked me to embrace her ("Embrace me!" she said. "Now!"), I was overjoyed. We looked into each other's eyes and, like two rivers flowing together, our souls were united. Outside the rain pelted against the windows, on the roof. I interpreted the rain, which was the resurgence of the whole world, as a panic extension of our love.

But my emotion did not keep me from discovering that Montero had contaminated Pauline's conversation. Sometimes when she spoke, I had the unpleasant impression that I was listening to my rival. I recognized the characteristic heaviness of the phrase, the candid and laborious attempts to find the right word; I recognized, painfully, the undeniable vulgarity.

With an effort, I was able to control myself. I looked at her face, her smile, her eyes. It was Pauline herself, intrinsic and perfect. Nothing had really changed her.

Then, as I contemplated her image in the shadowy recesses of the mirror, within the dark border of wreaths, garlands, and angels, she seemed different. It was as if I had discovered another version of Pauline, as if I saw her in a new way. I gave thanks for the separation that had interrupted my habit of seeing her, but had returned her to me more beautiful than ever.

"I must go," said Pauline. "Julius is waiting for me."

I perceived a strange mixture of scorn and anguish in her voice. I thought unhappily, "In the old days Pauline would not have been untrue to anyone." When I looked up she was gone.

I waited for a moment; then I called her. I called her again.
I went down to the entrance and ran along the street. She was
nowhere in sight. I went back into the building, shivering. I
said to myself, "The shower cooled things off." But I noticed
that the street was dry.

Returning to my apartment, I saw that it was nine o'clock.
I did not feel like going out for dinner; I was afraid of
meeting someone I knew. I made some coffee. I drank two or
three cups and ate part of a piece of bread.

I did not even know when Pauline and I would see each
other again. I wanted to talk to her. I wanted to ask her to
clear up some of my doubts (doubts were tormenting me, but
I knew she could clear them up easily). Suddenly my ingrati-
tude startled me. Fate was offering me every happiness and I
was not satisfied. That afternoon had been the culmination
of both our lives. That was what it meant to Pauline, and to
me. That was the reason why I had not asked for any explanation. (To speak, to ask questions would have been, somehow, to differentiate ourselves.)

But waiting until the next day to see Pauline seemed impossible. With an intense feeling of relief I resolved to go to
Montero's house that very evening. Immediately afterward I
changed my mind. I could not do that without first speaking
to Pauline. I decided to look for a friend—Louis Albert
Morgan seemed to be the logical one—and ask him to tell me
what he knew about Pauline's life during my absence from
Buenos Aires.

Then it occurred to me that the best thing would be simply
to go to bed and sleep. When I had rested I would see
everything more clearly. And, besides, I was not in the mood
to hear anyone speak disparagingly of Pauline. Going to bed
was like being put into a torture chamber (perhaps I remembered my nights of insomnia, when merely to stay in bed was
a way to pretend not to be awake). I turned out the light.

I would not dwell on Pauline's actions any longer. I knew
too little to understand the situation. Since I was unable to

empty my mind and to stop thinking, I would take refuge in the memory of that afternoon.

I would continue to love Pauline's face even if I had found something strange and unnatural in her behavior. Her face was the same as always, the pure and marvelous face that had loved me before Montero made his abominable appearance in our lives. I said to myself, "There is a fidelity in faces that souls perhaps do not share."

Or had I been mistaken all along? Was I in love with a blind projection of my preferences and dislikes? Had I never really known Pauline?

I selected one image from that afternoon—Pauline standing in front of the dark, smooth depths of the mirror—and tried to evoke it. When I could see the image, I had a sudden revelation: my doubts were caused by the fact that I was forgetting Pauline. I had tried to concentrate on the contemplation of her image. But imagination and memory are capricious faculties: I could see her tousled hair, a fold of her dress, the vague semidarkness around her, but not Pauline.

Many images, animated by spontaneous energy, passed before my closed eyes. And then I made a discovery. The small horse of jade could be seen on Pauline's right, in a corner of the mirror, like something on the dark edge of an abyss.

At first I was not surprised; but after a few minutes I remembered that the figurine was not in my apartment. I had given it to Pauline two years ago.

I told myself that it was simply a superimposition of anachronous memories (the older one, of the horse; the more recent one, of Pauline). That explained it; my fears evaporated, and I should have gone to sleep. But then I had an outrageous, and in the light of what I was to learn later, a pathetic thought. "If I don't go to sleep soon," I reflected, "I'll look haggard tomorrow and Pauline won't find me interesting."

Soon I realized that my memory of the figurine in the bedroom mirror was completely inaccurate. I had never put it in the bedroom. The only place in my apartment it had ever been was in the living room (on the bookshelf or in Pauline's hands or in my own).

Terrified, I tried to conjure up those memories again. The mirror reappeared, outlined by angels and garlands of wood, with Pauline in the center and the little horse at the right side. I was not sure whether it reflected the room. Perhaps it did, but in a vague and summary way. On the other hand, the little horse was rearing splendidly on the shelf of the bookcase, which filled the whole background. A new person was hovering in the darkness at one side; I did not recognize him immediately. Then, with only slight interest, I noticed that I was that person.

I saw Pauline's face, in its totality. It seemed to be projected to me by the extreme intensity of her beauty and her despair. When I awoke I was crying.

It was impossible to judge how long I had been sleeping. But my dream was no invention. It was an unconscious continuation of my imaginings, and reproduced the scenes of the afternoon faithfully.

I looked at my watch. It was five o'clock. I would get up early and, even at the risk of making Pauline angry, go to her house. That decision, however, did not relieve my anguish perceptibly.

I got up at seven-thirty, took a long bath, and dressed slowly.

I did not know where Pauline lived. The janitor at my building let me borrow his telephone book and city directory. Neither listed Montero's address. I looked for Pauline's name; it was not listed either. Then I discovered that someone else was living at Montero's former residence. I thought I would ask Pauline's parents for the address.

I had not seen them for a long time, not since I found out

that Pauline loved Montero. Now, to explain, I would have to tell them how much I had suffered. I did not have the courage.

I decided to talk to Louis Albert Morgan. I could not go to his house before eleven. I wandered through the streets in a daze, pausing to speculate on the shape of a molding, or pondering on the meaning of a word heard at random. I remember that at Independence Square a woman, with her shoes in one hand and a book in the other, was walking up and down on the damp grass in her bare feet.

Morgan received me in bed, drinking from an enormous bowl which he held with both hands. I caught a glimpse of a whitish liquid with a piece of bread floating on the surface.

"Where does Montero live?" I asked.

He had finished drinking the milk, and was fishing bits of bread from the bottom of the cup.

"Montero is in jail," he replied.

I could not conceal my amazement.

"What?" Morgan continued. "Didn't you know?"

He undoubtedly imagined that I knew everything except that one detail, but because he liked to talk he told me the whole story. I thought that I was going to faint, that I had fallen suddenly into a pit; and there, too, I heard the ceremonious, implacable, and precise voice that related incomprehensible facts with the monstrous and unquestioning conviction that they were already known to me.

This is what Morgan told me: Suspecting that Pauline would come to visit me the day before I left for Europe, Montero hid in the garden. He saw her come out; he followed her; he overtook her in the street. When a crowd began to gather, he forced her to get into a taxi. They drove around all night along the shore and out by the lakes, and early the next morning he shot her to death in a hotel in the suburbs. That had not happened yesterday; it had happened the night before I left for Europe; it had happened two years ago.

In life's most terrible moments we tend to fall into a kind of protective irresponsibility. Instead of thinking about what is happening to us, we focus our attention on trivialities.

At that moment I asked Morgan, "Do you remember the last party I gave before I went to Europe?"

Morgan said that he did.

"When you noticed I was concerned, and you went to my bedroom to call Pauline, what was Montero doing?" I asked.

"Nothing," replied Morgan briskly. "Nothing. Oh, now I remember. He was looking at himself in the mirror."

I went back to my apartment. In the entrance hall I met the janitor. Affecting indifference, I asked if he knew that Miss Pauline had died.

"Why, of course!" he said. "It was in all the papers. The police even came here to question me." The man looked at me curiously. "Are you all right? Do you want me to help you upstairs?" he asked.

I said no, and hurried up to my apartment. I have a vague memory of struggling with the key; of picking up some letters under the door; and of throwing myself face down on my bed.

Later, I was standing in front of the mirror thinking, "I am sure that Pauline visited me last night. She died knowing that her marriage to Montero had been a mistake—an atrocious mistake—and that we were the truth. She came back from death to complete her destiny, our destiny." I remembered a sentence that Pauline had written in a book years ago: "Ours have already been united." I kept thinking, "Last night it finally happened, at the moment when I made love to her." Then I told myself, "I am unworthy of her. I have doubted, I have been jealous. She came back from death to love me."

Pauline had pardoned me. Never before had we loved each other so much. Never before had we been so close to each other.

I was still under the spell of that sad and triumphant

intoxication of love when I wondered—or rather, when my brain, accustomed to the habit of proposing alternatives, wondered—whether there was another explanation for the visit of the previous night. Then, like a thunderbolt, the truth came to me.

Now I wish I could find that I am mistaken again. Unfortunately, as always happens when the truth comes out, my horrible explanation clarifies the things that seemed mysterious. They, in turn, confirm the truth.

Our wretched love did not draw Pauline from her grave. There was no ghost of Pauline. What I embraced was a monstrous ghost of my rival's jealousy.

The key to it all is found in Pauline's visit to me the night before I sailed for Europe. Montero followed her and waited for her in the garden. He quarreled with her all night long, and because he did not believe her explanations—but how could he have doubted her integrity?—he killed her the next morning.

I imagined him in jail, brooding about her visit to me, picturing it to himself with the cruel obstinacy of his jealousy.

The image that entered my apartment was a projection of Montero's hideous imagination. The reason I did not discover it then was that I was so touched and happy that I desired only to follow Pauline's bidding. And yet there were several clues. One was the rain. During the visit of the real Pauline—the night before I sailed—I did not hear the rain. Montero, in the garden, felt it directly on his body. When he imagined us, he thought that we had heard it. That is why I heard the rain last night. And then I found that the street was dry.

The figurine is another clue. I had it in my apartment for just one day: the day of my party. But for Montero it was like a symbol of the place. That is why it appeared last night.

I did not recognize myself in the mirror because Montero

did not imagine me clearly. Nor did he imagine the bedroom with precision. He did not really know Pauline. The image projected by Montero behaved in a way that was unlike Pauline and, what is more, it even talked like him.

The fantasy Montero invented is his torment. My torment is more real. It is the certainty that Pauline did not come back to me because she was disenchanted in her love. It is the certainty that she never really loved me at all. It is the certainty that Montero knew about aspects of her life that I have heard others mention obliquely. It is the certainty that when I embraced her—in the supposed moment of the union of our souls—I obeyed a request from Pauline that she never made to me, one that my rival had heard many times.

Translated from the Spanish by Roth L.C. Sims

Other Titles In This Series

The Day is Dark and Three Travellers
Marie-Claire Blais

Resident Alien
Clark Blaise

Nine Men Who Laughed
Austin Clarke

Café Le Dog
Matt Cohen

Intimate Strangers: New Stories from Quebec
edited by Matt Cohen and Wayne Grady

High Spirits
Robertson Davies

The Times Are Never So Bad
Andre Dubus

Voices from the Moon and Other Stories
Andre Dubus

The Pool in the Desert
Sara Jeannette Duncan

Other Titles In This Series

The Tatooed Woman
Marian Engel

Dinner Along the Amazon
Timothy Findley

Something Out There
Nadine Gordimer

Fables of Brunswick Avenue
Katherine Govier

The Penguin Book of Canadian Short Stories
edited by Wayne Grady

Treasure Island
Jean Howarth

The Moccasin Telegraph and Other Stories
W. P. Kinsella

The Thrill of the Grass
W. P. Kinsella

Champagne Barn
Norman Levine

Learning by Heart
Margot Livesey

Other Titles In This Series

Dark Arrows: Chronicles of Revenge
collected by Alberto Manguel

Evening Games: Chronicles of Parents and Children
collected by Alberto Manguel

Tales from Firozsha Baag
Rohinton Mistry

Darkness
Bharati Mukherjee

The Moons of Jupiter
Alice Munro

The Street
Mordecai Richler

Melancholy Elephants
Spider Robinson

The Light in the Piazza
Elizabeth Spencer

The Stories of Elizabeth Spencer
Elizabeth Spencer

Goodbye Harold, Good Luck
Audrey Thomas